GET ALL THIS FREE

WITH JUST ONE PROOF OF PURCHASE:

$50 VALUE

◆ **Hotel Discounts** up to 60% at home and abroad ◆ **Travel Service** - Guaranteed lowest published airfares plus 5% cash back on tickets ◆ **$25 Travel Voucher** ◆ **Sensuous Petite Parfumerie** collection ◆ **Insider Tips Letter** with sneak previews of upcoming books

You'll get a FREE personal card, too. It's your passport to all these benefits– and to even more great gifts & benefits to come!

There's no club to join. No purchase commitment. No obligation.

SR-PP5A

Enrollment Form

☐ *Yes!* I WANT TO BE A *Privileged Woman*.
Enclosed is one *PAGES & PRIVILEGES*™ Proof of
Purchase from any Harlequin or Silhouette book currently for
sale in stores (Proofs of Purchase are found on the back pages
of books) and the store cash register receipt. Please enroll me
in *PAGES & PRIVILEGES*™. Send my Welcome Kit and FREE
Gifts -- and activate my FREE benefits -- immediately.

More great gifts and benefits to come.

NAME (please print)

ADDRESS   APT. NO

CITY   STATE   ZIP/POSTAL CODE

PROOF OF PURCHASE
SAMPLE ONLY

**NO CLUB!
NO COMMITMENT!**
*Just one purchase brings
you great Free Gifts and
Benefits!*

Please allow 6-8 weeks for delivery. Quantities are limited. We reserve the right to
substitute items. Enroll before October 31, 1995 and receive one full year of benefits.

Name of store where this book was purchased_____

Date of purchase_____

Type of store:
    ☐ Bookstore   ☐ Supermarket   ☐ Drugstore
    ☐ Dept. or discount store (e.g. K-Mart or Walmart)
    ☐ Other (specify)_____

Which Harlequin or Silhouette series do you usually read?

_____

Complete and mail with one Proof of Purchase and store receipt to:
U.S.: *PAGES & PRIVILEGES*™, P.O. Box 1960, Danbury, CT 06813-1960
Canada: *PAGES & PRIVILEGES*™, 49-6A The Donway West, P.O. 813,
North York, ON M3C 2E8

SR-PP5B

"Are you married or something?

I mean, are you meeting someone inside?" Trent said.

Rae gave a rueful smile. "I was 'or something,' but he canceled our plans for today."

Trent frowned. "I hope he had a good excuse for letting you attend a wedding alone."

Rae's smile widened. "The best. He's the groom."

Trent's eyebrows shot up, but he offered her his elbow. "Join me?" he asked softly.

Rae was clearly charmed. He returned her appraising look and laughed. "*I'll* never get trapped by the bonds of matrimony," he pronounced. "When it comes to walking down the aisle, I'm the immovable object."

Rae's smile brought out her dimples. "Really? Folks around here think I'm the irresistible force."

She ducked into the church. And, eerily enough, Trent found himself drawn irresistibly after her. Down the aisle. To the strains of organ music...

Dear Reader,

This month, take a walk down the aisle with five couples who find that a MAKE-BELIEVE MARRIAGE can lead to love that lasts a lifetime!

Beloved author Diana Palmer introduces a new LONG, TALL TEXAN in *Coltrain's Proposal*. Jeb Coltrain aimed to ambush Louise Blakely. Her father had betrayed him, and tricking Louise into a fake engagement seemed like the perfect revenge. Until he found himself wishing his pretend proposal would lead to a real marriage.

In Anne Peters's *Green Card Wife*, Silka Olsen agrees to marry Ted Carstairs—in name only, of course. Silka gets her green card, Ted gets a substantial fee and everyone is happy. Until Silka starts having thoughts about Ted that aren't so practical! This is the first book in Anne's FIRST COMES MARRIAGE miniseries.

In *The Groom Maker* by Debut author Lisa Kaye Laurel, Rachel Browning has a talent for making grooms out of unsuspecting bachelors. Yet, *she's* never a bride. When Trent Colton claims he's immune to matrimony, Rachel does her best to make him her own Mr. Right.

You'll also be sure to find more love and laughter in *Dream Bride* by Terri Lindsey and *Almost A Husband* by Carol Grace.

And don't miss the latest FABULOUS FATHER, Karen Rose Smith's *Always Daddy*. We hope you enjoy this month's selections and all the great books to come.

Happy Reading!

Anne Canadeo
Senior Editor, Silhouette Romance

Please address questions and book requests to:
Silhouette Reader Service
U.S.: 3010 Walden Ave., P.O. Box 1325, Buffalo, NY 14269
Canadian: P.O. Box 609, Fort Erie, Ont. L2A 5X3

THE GROOM MAKER

Lisa Kaye Laurel

Silhouette

ROMANCE™

Published by Silhouette Books

America's Publisher of Contemporary Romance

To Rick, first and always,
for sharing a wonderful life.

And for her inspiration,
my thanks to Barbara Delinsky.

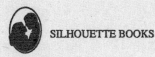 SILHOUETTE BOOKS

ISBN 0-373-19107-3

THE GROOM MAKER

Copyright © 1995 by Lisa Rizoli

This edition published by arrangement with Harlequin Books S.A.

® and TM are trademarks of Harlequin Books S.A., used under license.
Trademarks indicated with ® are registered in the United States Patent
and Trademark Office, the Canadian Trade Marks Office and in other
countries.

Printed in U.S.A.

LISA KAYE LAUREL

has worked in a number of fields, but says that nothing she's done compares to the challenges—and rewards—of being a full-time mom. Her extra energy is channeled into creating stories. She counts writing high on her list of blessings, which is topped by the love and support of her husband, her son, her daughter, her mother and her father.

Rae & ~~Mason~~

~~Kevin~~
~~Anthony~~ ~~Little Ed~~
~~Keith~~
~~Joel~~ ~~Larry~~
~~Nathaniel~~
~~Joshua~~
~~Adam~~ ~~Dennis~~
~~Jim~~

... Trent?

Chapter One

Rachel Browning twisted the taps, then tore off her clothes while the ancient plumbing cursed and whined. As soon as the hot water hit the pipes, she was in the shower. The wedding was starting in twenty minutes. She would be ready in time—barely—unless the groom decided he had to see her before the ceremony.

With more volume than finesse, she began to hum the "Wedding March" over the erratic spurting of the water as she lathered up her washcloth.

Suddenly a deep masculine voice cut into the big finale of her song. "What's going on in there?"

Startled, Rae almost lost her footing in the slippery old tub. Instinctively, she grabbed the shower curtain and wrapped it around her. Water began to leak out onto the worn linoleum floor.

Then she realized that the voice was coming from outside the bathroom window, which was inconveniently placed right in the wall of the shower. Here comes the groom, she thought with a sigh. No one else would have the nerve to come up to that window. He always had hated her singing. And his timing had always been off. She let the shower curtain fall back into place, mentally calculating how many minutes late she would be for the wedding now that she had to sop water up off the bathroom floor.

"The usual thing that goes on in a shower," she answered. "Where have you been? I waited as long as I could. It's too late now, even for a quickie."

There was a long pause. "Does that mean you usually have time for a quickie when men come calling at your bathroom window?" The low male voice continued, muffled by the sound of the shower.

An eerie suspicion prickled its way slowly up Rae's spine. "Cut it out, Jim. You don't have time for joking. You'd better get to the church."

There was another pause. Rae ran the washcloth over her body as fast as she could. Something was giving her the creeps, and being naked in the shower was not a position of strength. Maybe she had been too hasty in assuming that it was Jim out there.

She had been. The voice came back through the window at her, low and disturbing. "This isn't Jim. Who *are* you?"

"Who are *you*?" Rae countered, goose bumps texturing her skin despite the warmth of the water falling on her.

"I happen to be the owner of this house. Which makes me more than a little curious about what a strange woman is doing in my shower."

Rae blew out a gust of breath. Not a criminal or a psycho. Just the owner of the house.

Wait a minute. This house, where she lived and had her hair salon, belonged to her friend Maureen Peters's son, who was a hotel executive in Tokyo. He had inherited the house years ago and left it to the care of his mother, who had a gift boutique in it. What was he doing here?

Rae bit her lip, as she shampooed her hair, trying to recall the name of a man she had never met. Then she remembered that he had been named after his father, Maureen's first husband. "Thomas?" she said suddenly.

"You seem to know my name, but I still don't know yours."

She stuck her head under the spray, beginning the long process of rinsing shampoo out of her thick, shoulder-length hair with this woefully low water pressure. "I'm Rae," she said, as though that explained everything.

There was no reply. After a while she said, "You do know who I am . . . don't you?"

"No. But I am interested—*very* interested—in finding out. And while you're at it, you can tell me why my key doesn't work anymore, and what that new sign by the front door is all about."

Had Maureen never told him about her? Highly unlikely. Rae's instincts told her to try to smooth over the awkward situation, despite the fact that she didn't like the intimacy of talking to a strange man while she showered a few feet away from where he stood. The wide-open, first-floor window and its waterproof—and hopefully, opaque—curtain were all that was between them.

Resolutely, she went on. "The sign out front is for my hair salon, Styles. Your mother had the lock changed when the doorknob broke last year." She paused as some water sloshed onto her face. "And I'm here because I have an agreement with your mother. I was under the impression that you knew about it. Maybe you should talk to her. Now, if you will excuse me, I'd like to finish my shower."

Even over the racket of the pipes, she could hear the tightness in his low voice.

"Enjoy it. I expect it will be the last one you'll take in my house."

After a few minutes of quiet, Rae pulled a corner of the window curtain aside and looked out into the empty side yard. There was not a sign of the man who had so mysteriously appeared and so suddenly posed a threat to her happiness.

Rae was still a block away when she heard the cheery peal of bells filling the fresh May air, signaling the start of the wedding ceremony. She was late. As she rushed along the empty sidewalk, a man walked around the corner from the church parking lot and headed in her direction. A hope flashed through her that it was not Thomas. She was sure to meet up with him, but Rae wanted Maureen there.

In front of the church steps she paused, her attention captured by the man who approached. She had never seen him before, and in the three years that she had lived there, she had come to know everyone in the town of Emerson. He must be an out-of-town wedding guest. Facing the sun, Rae couldn't see the man's face, but his silhouette was long and lean, and his long strides complemented his taut, athletic build. He wore his sport jacket with casual grace, its hunter green color doing as much for his sandy brown hair as the afternoon sun glinting off it and the wind lightly ruffling it. Rae, who touched people's hair day in and day out in her work, was surprised to find her fingers itching to test the rich texture of his.

A few yards short of her, the man slowed, and Rae quickly came to her senses and realized that she was both late for the wedding and ogling a man. A handsome man, true, but a total stranger. She turned toward the church, and he fell into step beside her. His voice was low and pleasant.

"Excuse me, but are you going to the wedding?"

Rae stopped. "Yes."

"I'm Trent Colton. Friend of the groom."

Not Thomas, owner of the house. Rae breathed a sigh of relief as she held out her hand. "Rachel Browning. Friend of both."

"Are you alone?" he asked.

Rae looked up and down the sidewalk, deserted but for them. "I believe I am."

"I meant, are you meeting someone inside?" he said, smiling. "Are you married or something?"

She gave a rueful smile back. "I was 'or something,' but he canceled our plans for today."

He frowned. "I hope he had a good excuse for letting you attend a wedding alone."

Almost imperceptibly, her smile widened. "The best. He's the groom."

His eyebrows shot up, but he betrayed no other emotion. Instead, he offered her his elbow. "Join me?" he asked softly.

Rae was charmed. "Thank you," she said, placing her hand on his forearm, which was solid and muscular under the jacket. "And please, don't hold it against Jim. He made the right choice."

"Jim's got a lot of explaining to do," he said with a smile as he walked her up the church steps. "He and I once vowed that we'd never get trapped by the bonds of matrimony."

Rae slanted a wise look up at him. "It seems to me that most men talk a good game about resisting marriage, then end up happy to walk down the aisle with the right woman."

He gave a bitter laugh. "Then I'm not like most men."

At the top of the stairs, she turned toward him and studied his face. Under eyebrows that matched his sandy hair, his hazel eyes should have looked playful. But they were inscrutably deep. Intuitively, Rae knew he was right. He wasn't like any man she had ever met in her life.

He returned her appraising look. "You have to understand that I have my reasons," he said, his tone gentler, but just as firm. "When it comes to walking down the aisle, I'm the immovable object."

Slowly, the corners of Rae's mouth curled up in a smile that brought out the dimples in her curved cheeks. "Really? How interesting. You see, folks here seem to think that I'm the irresistible force."

She ducked into the church door, and eerily enough, he found himself drawn irresistibly after her down the aisle, to the strains of organ music.

Rae loved weddings. It was hard to concentrate on this one, though. The pew she had slipped into at the back of the church seemed unaccountably full, although she and Trent Colton were the only ones in it. Every time he shifted on the hard wooden seat, she felt the vibrations to her innermost core. When he held the hymnal for them both, the feel of his arm against hers made it hard for her to read the words. Meeting a handsome stranger at a wedding was every woman's fantasy. It took a while for Rae to adjust to the idea that it was really happening to her.

Then, too, the sudden appearance of Maureen Peters's son, Thomas, and his surprise at her being in his house were never far from her mind. She had to find Maureen and talk to her as soon as possible. Right after the ceremony.

Still, the words of love floating up from the front of the sanctuary penetrated her haze and, as such words never failed to do, moved her to tears. As she began to search her purse for a tissue, she felt a handkerchief being pressed into her hand. Trent Colton looked thoughtfully away after she took it. He had the smooth manners of a sophisticated man of the world. Momentarily, Rae wondered what a man who vowed never to marry thought about a sap who cried at weddings.

When the ceremony ended, the wedding party marched past them down the wide center aisle of the church. The people in the front pews started to shuffle out after them. Rae searched the crowd for Maureen. Then she saw her friend's auburn hair, tinted gently with silver, and waved to her. The torturously slow line finally dragged itself forward until Maureen was at their pew.

"Maureen, I've got to talk to you," Rae said, then stopped. Her friend wasn't even looking at her. She was looking at the man standing next to her, a wide smile lighting up her attractive face. The next moment she launched herself into his arms.

Rae was taken aback at first, wondering how her friend knew this stranger. Then she remembered that Trent Colton had said he was a friend of the groom. Maybe he had lived in Emerson at one time.

Maureen pulled herself from the embrace and looked up at him. "We have a lot of catching up to do," she said, her voice shaky with emotion.

"That is an understatement," he said, smiling warmly.

Then Maureen turned to Rae. "I wanted to introduce you to my son myself, but I see you've already met him."

"Your son? Well, yes, in a manner of speaking," Rae said, thinking of Thomas's voice interrupting her shower. "Believe me, there was no formal introduction. It was quite a…surprise. Maureen, we've got to talk."

"Formal introduction? Rae, you're the friendliest person I know. Since when did you need a formal introduction to a man you've been sitting next to for the past hour?" Maureen said over her shoulder as the line moved suddenly forward, taking her along with it.

Rae looked up at the man next to her. She knew what *flabbergasted* meant, but she had never experienced the feeling until that moment. "You…you can't be Thomas Peters," she sputtered. "You said your name was Trent Colton!"

"Actually, it's Thomas Trent Colton, Jr. My mother's last name was Colton, too, until she married Hal Peters a few years ago," he said evenly.

Of course, Rae thought. How silly of her not to have remembered that Maureen had remarried.

"Everyone in this town calls me 'Trent.' And apparently I'm not the only one who goes by a nickname, Rachel. Or is it 'Rae'?" People standing in the aisle began to glance at them curiously. Not for the first time that afternoon, Trent had to struggle to retain his customary composure.

Rae took a deep breath and spoke in a low voice. "I'm having a hard time picturing you as the man who interrupted my shower."

"And I'm having a hard time figuring out why you were expecting to have a quickie with the groom a half hour before he married someone else," Trent shot back.

Rae's eyes widened in shock. "You can't think—" she spluttered, looking aghast. "I was going to give him a quickie *haircut!* Gosh sakes!"

"Of course. How could I forget? You are the woman who has turned my lovely country house into a hair salon." Trent made a concerted effort to tamp down his irritation. For one thing, the fact that he didn't know about her using his house seemed to be as big a shock to her as her being there was to him. For another, he needed to get the whole story from his mother.

And for still another, when he had come upon her on the church steps, he had found her extremely captivating. And despite this misunderstanding, he still did.

It was their turn to get into the receiving line. Rae seemed to be in a daze, so Trent grasped her shoulders and turned her toward the aisle, then followed her as she stumbled out of the church.

They were the last ones to go through the receiving line. The groom, a bearded man who resembled one of the larger species of bear, wasn't content with a kiss from Rae. He picked her up and spun her around in his arms. Several people standing nearby applauded.

"This wouldn't have happened if it hadn't been for you," Trent heard Jim say to her as he placed her on the ground again.

Rae gave him one of her warm smiles and said firmly, "Of course it would have, Jim Bruneski. You and Lynna are perfect together. I'm so glad you're both happy." Then she moved over to kiss the bride.

Trent stepped up in front of Jim. The two men looked at each other for several seconds in silence. Then, suddenly they came together in a hard hug.

"I'm glad you made it, buddy," Jim said gruffly as they pulled apart.

Trent put a hand to his ear. "What's that I hear? Must be the sound of hell freezing over. As I recall, that was when you said you would get married."

Jim shrugged, grinning. Then he gestured toward Rae. "Hey, are you with her?"

Trent paused for a minute. "I guess I am."

He watched as his friend's smile broadened. "Then I guess you're next," Jim said with a wink.

"What are you talking about?"

But Jim had already turned to escort his bride back into the church for photos. Trent decided he would have to find him later to get an explanation for that one. Right now, he needed to talk with his mother.

Maureen was waiting for him at the end of the receiving line, and when he reached her, she threw herself into his arms for another hug. Then he held her at arm's length, looking at her.

"It's great to see you again, Mom," he said, smiling at her. She looked even better than he remembered, and it was obvious why. She wasn't just happy—she was radiant, glowing from the inside out. He hadn't seen her looking that way often when he was growing up. Hal, her second husband, must be treating her a hell of a lot better than Trent's father had.

"Did you get my note?" she asked.

He nodded. After he had left Rae showering at his house, he had driven over to his mother's house. At least *that* key still worked, he thought wryly. Along with the note saying she'd see him at the wedding, Maureen had left him one of the new keys to his house.

"It was such a shock to get your message this morning that you'd be here for the wedding! How long will you be staying?"

"Three months."

Maureen's face lit up. "That long? Wonderful! Even though you never came here much when you lived in Boston, you've been so much farther away in Tokyo. It's so good to have you back. I can't believe it's been three years!"

"You look wonderful," Trent said. His mother had always had style. Buying jewelry and accessories for her gift boutique was second nature for her. "Your hair is different from the way I last saw it. I like it."

"Thank you. I'll pass along the compliment to Rae, of course. The woman is pure magic. We're so lucky to have her here."

Not exactly his reading of the situation, but now that the subject of Rae had been broached, Trent went with it. "How did you meet her?"

"Hal knew her father. When he was in the hospital a few years ago, Hal used to visit him. Rae was there whenever she wasn't at the hair salon where she worked. She mentioned to him that she wanted to go out on her own someday, and he told me about it." Maureen paused, smiling. "There was so much room at the house with just the boutique, I thought, why not here? After her father died, Hal brought her out here so we could meet each other, and she's been here ever since."

"What sort of arrangement do you have with her about the house?" Trent said.

"Why, Trent, I told you all about it on the phone when it happened, three years ago. She takes care of the lawn and garden as payment for housing her business there."

Trent had a fuzzy recollection of a rushed conversation that had taken place when he had first arrived in Tokyo. He hadn't paid much attention, because in exchange for having her gift boutique there, his mother had taken care of details at the house for him ever since his grandparents had left it to him, while he was still in college. But he had hung up the phone under the impression that his mother had hired some guy named Ray to do the outdoor maintenance, and assumed that "housing the business" there meant that the guy was storing his lawn mower, rake and spade in the shed out back.

"Trent, is there some problem? Because I distinctly remember you saying at the time that you didn't need to know about details like that, and I should do whatever I thought was best."

It sounded like something he would have said. It was certainly how he felt. "You've looked after the place for me for a long time, and I appreciate that," he said. "It looks great." Apparently Rae's cutting magic worked with hedge shears, too.

"Rae keeps the inside nice, too."

"Is that part of the arrangement?" He had better find out all the particulars, so he knew what he was working with.

"No, she does that on her own. Living there and all."

"I see." No wonder she had been taking a shower there. She *lived* there. Just having her salon there wasn't complicating things enough, Trent thought.

"I didn't think you'd mind. You were halfway around the world, and Rae needed a place to stay," Maureen said reasonably. "I thought it would be better if the house was occupied, anyway."

Trent hung on to his calm. Living there, working there, it didn't really matter. What mattered was that she was there. "When does the lease you signed with her expire?"

"Lease? Oh, we didn't sign anything, Trent. It was a verbal agreement. Our understanding is that she can be in the house rent-free for the next two years, until you come home from Tokyo."

Trent set his jaw, but didn't say anything.

"What is it?"

"My plans have changed. I know I said I'd be in Tokyo for five years, but I was trying to prepare you for the worst. The actual contract I signed was for three years with an option for an additional two. My three years are up, and I've decided not to take the option. When you told me you were retiring and closing the boutique, it sealed my decision."

"You're staying? That's wonderful!" Maureen beamed. "I always pictured you settling down in that house someday."

"Settling down? Me?" Trent had to laugh at that one. "Mom, I'm going to sell the house."

Maureen looked shocked. "What? *Why?*"

"I'm going to open a hotel in Boston. Small, but all my own."

Maureen's smile reappeared. "Congratulations. I always hated the thought of you working for a big, impersonal corporation that would ship you halfway around the world."

Trent grinned. "They didn't kidnap me. They made an offer. A good offer. And I accepted."

"Well, you're back now, and that's the important thing," his mother said, with a satisfied-sounding note in her voice. "But don't you want to hang on to the house?"

Trent shook his head. "To raise the capital I need to buy my hotel, I have to sell the house."

"Why not sell that condo you have in Boston? You could live here in Emerson and commute to your hotel."

"For one thing, the condo wouldn't bring enough money, and for another, it would be much more convenient to live right in Boston than way out here."

Maureen frowned thoughtfully. "Aren't you renting your condo out?"

"Yes, but the lease is up in three months, so I'll move back in then. That's when the house is going to be sold, too, and I'll take possession of my hotel."

"You're selling the house in *three months?* But Rae will be there for two more years." Maureen paused, and gradually a look of understanding spread across her face. "Oh, I get it. That's the problem, isn't it?

You want her out now. But Trent, that would break my agreement with her!''

"Let's not assume the worst. After all, Rae might *want* to move out," Trent ventured.

"Not a chance," Maureen said firmly. "Trent, I'm sorry this situation conflicts with your plans, but Rae has plans, too, and she is expecting to be able to stay where she is for two more years. I wish you had said something when I first told you about her."

So did he. "Well, I didn't," he said flatly. "I'll have to work something out with Rae."

It didn't make Trent feel any better to know that he was holding all the cards. His mother's agreement was a verbal one, and he was sure that, legally, he had every right to force Rae to vacate. But he didn't want to have to do that. If only Rae would agree to leave willingly, everyone would be happy. But if what his mother said was true, that appeared unlikely to happen.

Maureen left to find her husband, Hal. All of the guests were starting to clear off the church lawn and head for the reception. Trent looked around for Rae, and saw her about to get into a car at the curb. He walked up behind her and put a hand on her shoulder.

Rae whipped around. "You startled me!" she said, as her heart started thumping in her chest.

"Just wanted to get your attention," he said. He leaned over and closed the car door, waving for the driver to go on without her.

He had her attention, all right, Rae thought. How could he not? The man positively exuded male magnetism. From the top of his wind-roughened hair all the way down to the soles of his shoes, his presence was consuming.

"It's time for us to head over to the reception," he said.

Rae had to look up to meet his eyes. "You mean you want to go together?"

He had intended to take this time to talk with her about the house, but seeing her standing there looking up at him, so beautiful, and so...sweet, he decided that could wait. "I asked you to join me," he reminded her, smiling as he held out his arm. "Do you mind walking?"

"Not at all." As she took his arm, Rae felt her optimism return. If there was some problem about her staying in the house, he would hardly want to be her escort. She had seen him talking to Maureen and guessed that she had answered whatever questions he had.

They were the only ones walking the short distance to the reception, and when they started to cross the town green, Rae stopped. "Would you mind turning around for a moment?"

Although curious about her odd request, Trent did as she asked. Behind him, he could hear rustling sounds.

"Ah. That feels *wonderful*," Rae said, with a soft sigh of deep satisfaction.

"May I look now?" Trent had walked across the town green with his buddies, his mother, his grandparents and dates too numerous to count, but this was the first time one of them had stopped and asked him to turn his back.

"Yes."

"Then let's go." He turned to face her, and sucked in a quick, audible breath.

She was barefoot, her shoes dangling from one hand, while the other was busy stuffing what looked like nylons into her purse. He blinked. And in that split second one startling fact became all too clear.

He was undeniably, achingly, attracted to this woman.

Rae shook her head gently, the unconscious movement of a woman whose dark hair is confined to a sophisticated twist at the back of her head only for special occasions. Swept up like that, it provided a dramatic frame for her fair-skinned face with its delicate brows arched over eyes of coffee brown. He found himself wondering what her hair would look like falling down loose, silky and full, over the smooth skin of her shoulders.

She set a course directly toward the house of Jim's parents, where the reception was to be held, shunning the path to walk in the softly greening grass. After a moment she stopped to look back toward where he stood rooted to the town green like the great trees that had shaded generations of Emerson townspeople. "Mr. Colton," she called, her tentative smile hinting at the dimples that nestled in both cheeks. "Are you ready?"

"Yes," he said. It was a lie. He wasn't at all ready to deal with a woman who had singlehandedly iced his plans and set his libido ablaze.

She seemed blithely unconcerned about her bare calves and feet. While he, on the other hand, was intensely aware of them.

They were smooth, glossy and shapely. Touchable.

He brought his hand to his own face, drawing it across his beard stubble, as if the contrast might bring him to his senses. He caught up to Rae, and she turned to him, her face radiant with pleasure.

"There's something so compelling about a day this beautiful." She took a deep breath and let it out with a sigh.

He knew what she meant. There was something very compelling about her, as well, he thought as he fell into step beside her, wanting to walk barefoot the way she did.

He didn't, although her innocent sensuality made him consider it. He just took a deep breath and savored being with the attractive—and curious—woman whose soft smile spoke to him like none of the signs of nature she gloried in pointing out during their walk. Like nothing had ever spoken to him before.

They reached the sidewalk at the other side of the green, and Rae balanced on each foot in turn, slipping her shoes back on. When she wobbled, he caught her by the elbow, and it took him a fraction of a second longer than he liked to release her again. She gave him another of those wonderfully warm smiles.

Then her brow wrinkled in thought. "Mr. Colton, I..."

"Please, call me 'Trent.'"

She hesitated. She liked the distance of calling him "Mr. Colton," even though he didn't have more than a few years on her.

His voice was gently persuasive. "Everyone here does, Rachel. Or should I call you 'Rae'?"

"Everyone here does," she said, with a half smile. "Rae was my childhood nickname, but somehow it feels right here in Emerson."

"It fits you."

That was what her father had always said. He used to call her his "Rae of sunshine." She cleared her throat. "I think we should talk about the house. I gather that my being there was somewhat of a shock for you."

She was direct—he'd give her that. No player of games was Rae. He came back at her with the same honesty. "As shocking as my sudden appearance must have been for you," he said. "My mother had told me about your arrangement, but frankly, I didn't pay attention to the details at the time. It's obvious that you've done a wonderful job on the lawn and gardens."

Rae relaxed, and the creases on her forehead smoothed out again. "Then it's all right? Oh, I can't tell you what this means—"

He held up his hand. "Please, there's something you need to know. I would have no objection to your business being there, or to your living there, except for one thing."

"What's that?"

"I'm selling the house."

Rae suddenly felt her knees go rubbery. "Selling . . . the house?"

"Yes."

"Well, I suppose that could take a while. Years, maybe," she said, sounding hopeful.

He shook his head. "Months. The timing for my plans has coincided nicely with my mother's decision to retire and close the boutique."

"But Maureen and I agreed that my salon and I could stay there two more years, even though the boutique is closing."

Trent's voice gentled. "I'm sorry now that I didn't stay in closer communication with my mother. I'd like to be able to honor her agreement with you, but I don't see how I can. There's no possible way I can keep the house for two more years."

"You want me to move out." Rae's voice sounded to her as though it were coming from very far away. Nothing seemed real about the conversation.

"What I want is to buy my own hotel, and I need the money from the sale of the house to do it. Unfortunately, that means you will have to leave," he said. "I'm sorry, Rae, but my hands are tied. I've had the amazing good fortune to locate the hotel I want to buy, and to find an interested buyer for the house. The plan is for both sales to go through in three months."

Rae felt the weight of his words settle around her. He wasn't the only one who had a plan, and hers was being sent into a tailspin. Leave? She had come to Emerson to build a business of her own, and with a lot of determination and very little money she was succeeding. Her reputation had gained her a loyal clientele, and all she needed now was a little more time to raise the capital she would need to put a down payment on a place of her own.

She *had* to stay at Trent's house. There wasn't another space in town that could house both her and her business, and she couldn't afford to pay rent both for her salon and for a place to live and still save enough for a down payment. And she *couldn't* leave Emerson, the town she loved and that had made her one of its own.

Because during the past three years, her dream had grown. She not only wanted her own salon, she wanted it in the town she had come to love, in the house she had come to love.

Trent's house.

Faced with losing it all, she felt her desperation surface, and with it, her courage. "So you believe that my agreement with your mother can be superseded by your plans? Legally?" She kept her tone excruciatingly matter-of-fact.

"You did have a prior agreement," he conceded. "Then again, it's not on paper. It seems to be a bit nebulous, legally speaking. I'm no lawyer, and neither are you. If we want to be real suckers, we can both spend our hard-earned money and let two legal eagles hash this out. We can go that route if you want." He fervently hoped that she didn't want. If this thing got tied up in the courts, it would never be settled in three months, and he'd lose his hotel and his buyer.

"No." Rae had a feeling that when the dust settled, he would win anyway, and she couldn't afford the legal fees. "But I don't want to move out, either," she said determinedly.

Trent was just as resolute. "I'd like to help you, Rae, but I don't see how I can."

"There has to be a way we can both get what we want," Rae said fiercely. "This just isn't fair!"

"We agree on that." He placed both hands on her arms and, in a voice full of understanding, said, "Look, we've both had quite a shock today."

He began to rub his hands gently up and down her arms from elbow to shoulder, and despite herself, Rae could feel herself relaxing.

"But important as working this thing out is to both of us," he continued, "I don't think Jim would forgive us if we missed his wedding reception."

His voice dropped a husky note as he added, "Unless I hear you say otherwise, I still consider myself your escort." And for the third time that afternoon, he held out his arm to her.

Chapter Two

Walking a block down Main Street cleared Rae's confusion about the house. Trent wanted her out, but staying in it was vital to her. She had an agreement with Maureen, and somehow, she was going to get him to honor it.

Walking a second block cleared her confusion about Trent. She couldn't deny that his charm appealed to her. She couldn't pretend that it didn't feel good to walk down the street with her arm in his, listening to his good-natured conversation and looking up at his killer smile. But she also couldn't help but wonder if he was turning his charm up a notch to try to get her to agree to move out of his house.

It was in her nature to be cooperative rather than confrontational, but she would be on her guard just in case. She would enjoy his pleasantries without succumbing to them.

He might end up winning, using fair means or foul, but she was not going to help him do it. There was no way he was going to charm her out of the house.

When they arrived at the reception, the party was in full swing. It looked as if the whole town had been invited, Trent thought, as he walked Rae up the front path. Rae took her hand off his arm as a group of women called her over, but Trent took gentle hold of her fingertips before she got away.

"Don't forget about me," he said in an undertone.

"I won't," she said, her brown eyes wide.

He registered their soft expression and allowed himself a small smile.

No sooner had Rae gone than Trent was enlisted to carry a picnic table over from the neighbor's yard. Carrying the other end of the table was Mason O'Hara, who was as tall, thin and thoughtful as he had been when Trent had taken business classes with him in high school. Shouldering both benches, a mountain of a man walked up beside Trent.

"Who the hell are you, stranger?" the man asked gruffly.

Trent grinned. "Well, if it isn't Little Ed Davis. It's been a long time."

"Long time, he says. Damn near thought you weren't ever coming home, you money-hungry, citified, womanizing son of a . . ." Little Ed dropped the benches and enveloped Trent in the kind of bear hug he used to give him after they had won football games.

And sometimes, after they'd lost. Trent had been quarterback, and Little Ed, at center, had saved his cookies more times than he cared to remember.

"Better than hanging around talking trash at the station all day," Trent said. His large, well-muscled friend now owned the family service station with his father, Big Ed, who was twice his son's age and half his size. "You're even uglier than I remember," he added for good measure.

Little Ed grinned back and pushed his overgrown red hair off his freckled face. "I ain't no pretty city boy, if that's what you mean."

Mason came around the picnic table to shake Trent's hand, then he, too, gave him a hug. "It's great to see you again," he said earnestly. "You'll have to meet my wife and kids."

Trent felt his jaw drop. Wife and kids. Plural. Mason? He cleared his throat. "Things sure have changed around here in a few short years. You're married, and now Jim's married. Looks like you and I are the only ones from the old gang who can go out nights, Little Ed."

Little Ed's laugh boomed out as he held up his left hand to Trent. A gold ring circled the third finger. "You'll have to do your tomcatting alone, old buddy," he said.

"You, too? I'd like to meet the woman who would sink so low as to marry the likes of you." In a strange sort of way, Trent felt betrayed. Somehow he had always assumed that no matter how far he went, how long he stayed away or how much he changed, things would always be the same back in sleepy old Emerson.

He had no right to feel that way, he told himself. After all, he had chosen to leave. First for college, then to work in Boston. The past three years in Tokyo, he had let the combined barriers of distance and time allow him to lose touch with his old friends.

"You just wait, and we'll fetch you the two most happily married women in Massachusetts," Little Ed vowed. He and Mason went off, leaving Trent to wander through the crowd, exchanging greetings with old classmates, neighbors, friends of his mother, parents of his friends. Everyone was smiling, joking, backslapping, handshaking. The handshakes were real, Trent noticed. Not like the business handshakes he received daily. The smiles were real, too.

None more so than Rae's. He saw her standing with the bridesmaids, laughing and chatting, and felt a pang of guilt. He knew she was upset about what was happening with the house, and he had left her hanging. Yet there she was, putting her personal problems aside to join in the celebration. The celebration of the marriage of a man, Trent suddenly remembered, who had only recently been dating her.

Just then, Rae glanced over and caught him looking at her. She looked flustered for a moment, but gave him an answering smile when he smiled at her. He noticed she wasn't drinking anything, so he gestured toward the glass in his hand. She nodded, still with that soft smile curling her lips, then went back to talking with the woman standing next to her.

Trent was baffled at the effect that small smile had on him. It was so soft, so innocent looking, not at all the kind of thing that usually made him hunger for a woman. He had always gone for fast-track career women, women who wanted to put as little into a relationship as he did. Women who never, ever gave a flip about commitment.

But Rae's sweet smile made him warm around the collar, the feel of the soft skin on her arms had raised goose bumps on his and a fleeting glimpse of the curve of her bare ankle, under a dress that was swirly full and longer than most, intrigued him more than he cared to admit.

He tried to assess Rae objectively. She had so much potential. As a lover, for one thing. He wondered if her hedonistic enjoyment of nature's wonders extended to the bedroom.

Wait a minute. A casual bed partner she was not— of that he was certain. She wasn't anything like the women who had drifted in and out of his life. Rae was the kind of woman a brother would blacken eyes over.

He cursed under his breath and went to the table where the drinks were, unhesitatingly pouring a lemonade for Rae before going to the keg to get a beer for himself. His instincts told him a woman like her didn't drink. When he found Rae, she was taking a sip of Little Ed's beer. Trent stood off a few paces, watching in fascination as she licked the foam from her lips, laughing as Little Ed walked away.

Trent approached, hesitating before handing her the lemonade. "I saw you drinking some of Little Ed's beer. Would you have preferred that?"

"No, I prefer lemonade," she said. "That was just for a taste. I haven't had beer from a keg since college."

"Real wild back then, were you?" he asked, hoping to dispel the effect her sweet innocence was having on him.

If she was offended by the dig, she didn't show it. "Not exactly," she said with a laugh. "I wasn't really a partyer. But I did have a taste for beer. I seem to have lost it, though, somewhere along the way."

Mason came up and introduced Trent to his wife, Michelle, whom he'd met at the computer software company where they worked, although Michelle had been home of late with toddler Davey and baby Alex. Mason confided to Trent with a proud smile that there was another one on the way. Then Little Ed lumbered up with his wife, Caroline, a petite beauty who had been head cheerleader in high school. Back then, she had only had eyes for Trent, but now she watched Little Ed adoringly as he cradled their infant daughter at his chest.

Rae knew them all, and looked more comfortable with the group than Trent felt. It was an alien experience for him, to be in the company of the wives—and offspring—of men with whom he'd always had an exclusively male relationship. His memory had freeze-framed them as they'd been the last time he had seen them. He was working to mentally fast-forward to the present. And he had to admit that both of his friends looked indecently happy.

And then there was Jim, who came over to endure, with good grace, the ribbing about the wedding night.

His bride, Lynna, who was wearing her mother's wedding gown, actually blushed. Trent had never before seen a blushing bride. He had always figured they were figments of overromantic imaginations.

"Food's ready, so come on over and help yourselves," Jim said. "I for one am going to make sure I get there before Little Ed does."

The buffet table was covered with a variety of mismatched dishes and platters filled with homemade food. It was a real old-fashioned New England potluck supper. Trent felt as though he had stumbled into a time warp. The last time he'd been to a wedding like this, he'd been as old as the little boys with clip-on ties who were chasing beribboned little girls around the rosebushes in the corner of the yard.

"There are kids at this wedding," he said out loud, as if he had just realized it.

Rae looked at him. "Is something wrong with that?"

"Not at all." Trent was glad the kids were there. They were having a ball. "But at all the weddings I've gone to in recent memory, children would have been about as welcome as the plague."

"How sad," Rae said, looking as if she meant it.

He carried his plate and Rae's to an empty table, and watched her get seated. She did so with a natural ease that couldn't have looked more breathtakingly graceful to Trent if she were settling upon the throne of England instead of on a picnic bench stained with old bird droppings in a backyard in Emerson. Their table soon filled up with an assortment of people, a number of whom had lived in the town for the better part of the century. It was nice seeing older folks at a wedding, too, Trent reflected, wondering if the time of the wedding, outrageously early by fashionable standards, had been set for the convenience of the young and old.

The high school jazz band, a group Jim had once played trumpet with, played background music that actually stayed at background noise level so people could converse while they ate. And the home-cooked food tasted better than most of the fancy sit-down meals Trent had eaten at country-club receptions.

"Are you always this quiet?" Rae asked, breaking in on his thoughts.

Trent turned to her with a smile that turned up one corner of his mouth. "Just taking in the scene. I haven't been here for quite a while."

"You were in Tokyo for three years, weren't you?"

"Yes. But I haven't lived in Emerson since I left for college."

Rae was astonished. "You haven't been back since then?"

"Visits, now and again."

"Has it changed much?"

"Emerson? Yes and no." In one way, it was the same as he remembered it, an anachronism in a world poised on the threshold of the twenty-first century. It made him feel all the more keenly how he himself had changed. But Trent didn't like introspection, so he focused, instead, on the woman beside him. He gave Rae his best smile. "Still the same people, but now their hair looks great."

Her eyes widened at first, then she burst into laughter. "If you're going to resort to shameless flattery to get me out of your house, Mr. Colton, I would think you'd be able to do better than that."

"It's the truth. My mom looks terrific. So do all her friends. The bride, the wedding party—yes, I heard you did their hair free—everyone looks great. It's not flattery—it's a compliment. And by the way, would it kill you to call me 'Trent'?"

She looked at him for the space of five heartbeats. Trent wondered why he was so aware of his heart beating strongly, and a little faster than usual.

Then she said, quietly, "Thank you for the compliment, Trent."

He leaned in close to her ear and said, "Now, if you want to hear shameless flattery, I'll be happy to oblige. Just as soon as I've gotten us seconds." He grabbed her plate and his and headed back to the buffet table.

While he was in line, a disc jockey replaced the jazz band and Jim and Lynna started off the dancing. Trent ate his seconds alone, because when he got back to the table Rae was up dancing with Mason. In fact, it seemed that everyone, young and old alike, was dancing. He watched Rae dance with Jim, Little Ed, Big Ed, Mason's son, Davey, and just about every other ineligible male in Emerson. In fact, now that Trent noticed, there weren't any eligible men in Emerson. Just married guys, and him. Pretty much a social wasteland for a beautiful young woman who was obviously the marrying kind.

"My son, not dancing?" Maureen slid onto the bench across from Trent.

He grinned at his mother. "Haven't seen anyone who could tempt me away from my plate till now. Would you do me the honor?"

"I thought you'd never ask."

He led her over to the patio, which was serving as a makeshift dance floor. "How have things been for you, Mom?"

"I can't complain. I've got the itch pretty bad, but—"

"The itch?"

"The grandmother itch. Happens to women my age."

"Oh, Mom." Trent pulled her closer. "I hate to have you wishing for the one thing I can't give you. Because no matter how much I want to see you happy, I can't see myself getting married and having a family."

"Now, I'm not complaining. After all, I'm your mother. I just want to see *you* happy. And I do get a vicarious thrill from holding my friends' grandbabies."

Of course. She was friends with most of his friends' mothers, and now they were all grandmothers. Or would be before long, Trent thought, noticing the tender way Jim was looking at Lynna as they danced by.

"How do you feel about retiring?" he asked his mother.

Maureen smiled. "I'm ready. Hal and I never took the time for a honeymoon when we got married, so we're having a ball making travel plans. And actually, when we get back, I'm thinking it would be fun to work part-time for Rae.''

Trent was silent.

"Trent? Would you mind if we switched partners? I haven't danced with Hal yet.''

Trent led her into her husband's arms, then danced away with Hal's partner. Rae.

"I ate my seconds without you," he said. "Ate yours, too, for that matter. When you stayed on the dance floor for the hokeypokey, I knew nothing would bring you back.''

"Oh, Trent, I'm sorry." Rae laughed. "But the Connor boy who delivers the newspaper asked me, and you know how fragile male egos are at his age.''

"Male egos are fragile at any age," he told her, but the flashing grin in his tanned face belied his words. A slow number came on, and he tightened his arm around her. "Now that you're all warmed up, I'm just glad to have a dance with my date.''

Rae was warmed up, all right. She wondered if she'd ever been so warmed up in her life. She wasn't the kind of woman who had ever described herself as hot for a man, so she wondered if the delicious warmth that was overtaking her was what it felt like. There was nothing in the world but the gentle pressure of his arms around her, the solid muscles of his chest as he pulled her closer. Her eyes drifted closed, the better to savor the sensations he evoked in her.

Trent wondered if he had ever held such sweetness in his arms. He knew the exact moment she relaxed and melted against him, making him ache in a place deep inside that he hadn't even known existed until then. Dancing had always been a perfunctory exercise for him, or a prelude to something else. But dancing with Rae was neither; it was a sensual pleasure in and of itself, and that indefinable something more. That scared the hell out of Trent. His body was spinning out of control, with a self-indulgent will of its own, but he kept his mind in focus.

His mind blamed this damn wedding for the alien feelings he was battling. The very atmosphere made it easy to be seduced by an enigmatic woman who was cleverly packaged as a dream come true. It made a man who had left no room for romance in his life wonder about happily ever after.

But Trent's parents had had a wedding like this, and theirs hadn't had a storybook ending. He mentally kept Rae at arm's length while he held her close.

Rae felt her partner tense almost imperceptibly, and came back to reality. She lifted her head up and looked at Trent. "Maybe we can reach some kind of a compromise."

"Hmm?"

"I mean about the house," Rae persisted. "Maybe your buyer wouldn't mind having a live-in caretaker."

"Not only is she eager to take possession, but she plans to turn the place into a restaurant. I'm afraid there would be no room for you or your salon."

"Oh." Rae tried a different approach. "It's none of my business, but your grandparents' place is more than just a house. It's special. Are you sure you want to sell it?"

He was silent for a minute. "I want that hotel," he said.

Rae felt her hopes for working out a new deal with him fade. He was set on selling now, so she was out. The timing stank. If it were two years from now, she would be making him an offer on the house herself.

"Look, Rae, I feel very badly about this situation, but you have to understand that jeopardizing this sale would not just affect an investment. It would affect my future," he said evenly. "I don't want to leave you high and dry, so you can stay in the house for the three months before the buyer and I pass papers. And if you want me to, I'll even help you look for a new location for your salon. Under the circumstances that's the best I can offer you."

The song came to an end, and so did Rae's hope that Trent would be able to honor his mother's agreement. As she pushed herself out of his arms, Jim stepped up to the microphone, with Lynna beside him.

"The two of us wouldn't be standing here, on the happiest day of our lives, if it wasn't for someone very special," he began.

Rae felt the pit of her stomach drop. This had happened at the past eleven weddings in Emerson, so she should have been ready for it this time, but once again it took her by surprise. She must have swayed a little, because Trent looked down at her with concern, then slung his arm around her shoulder.

Jim went on. "Before another minute goes by, we want all of you to join us in thanking Rae."

As the crowd around her began to applaud, Rae felt Trent's arm drop. A number of young couples, including Jim and Lynna, Little Ed and Caroline, Mason and Michelle and all of their parents, came up and hugged Rae, thanking her. She forced her widest smile as she accepted their attention.

When Trent caught her eye, he raised an eyebrow to question her. Rae went back to his side and gave him a wry smile. "'Rae' isn't the only nickname I have in this town."

"Really. What else do they call you?"

Rae took a deep breath. "The 'Groom Maker.'"

Trent looked at Rae, disbelieving. "They call you *what?*"

Jim broke in, grinning at his friend. "The 'Groom Maker,'" he repeated.

Trent said doubtfully, "I've heard of widow makers, but a *groom* maker? What is that supposed to mean?"

"It means that the twelve men Rae's dated in Emerson have all ended up married. To the women they went out with right after her," said Mason.

Trent looked at Rae. "Is this true?"

She shrugged. "When you do something that many times, you get a nickname."

"You mean, you're a *matchmaker?*" He sounded horrified, as if he'd found out she was a crystal-ball gazer, or something else as foreign to his business world. Maybe he was envisioning a tacky neon sign saying Grooms Made Here on his front door next to the Styles sign.

Rae tried to set him straight. "I don't make matches. I don't do anything. I just go out with the men, and they go off and marry other women. It's just some kind of odd coincidence.'' She had no idea why it happened, just that it did. And that she'd rather it didn't.

"It's a gift, I tell you. Twelve is too many times for it to be a coincidence,'' Little Ed's mother, Darlene, put in. She shifted her baby granddaughter, who lay sleeping in her arms. "I was a grandma wannabe, until Rae came along and went out with Little Ed. Now look at me. I'm a grandma for real!'' She beamed at Trent.

"But how?'' This was all a little too much for Trent to take on faith.

Mason's mother, Jeanne, who owned the bakery on Main Street, pulled him aside. "If it all sounds like magic, that's because it is. Rae has her own special brand of magic. After a few dates with her, Mason was brimming with confidence, Jim was a regular customer at the florist's and Little Ed was cleaning under his fingernails.''

Jim's mother chimed in, "If you want to know what I think, I think she's a cross between Knute Rockne and Emily Post. That's what I think.''

The minister came up and gave Rae a friendly handshake. "Thanks to my partner here, I've got the busiest wedding schedule and lowest divorce rate in the county. You bring me the loose ends and I tie the knot, right, Rae?''

Rae managed a weak smile, then looked to see how Trent was reacting to all this. His smile was broadening by the minute. He seemed to have gotten over his initial shock.

"So how long does it take this voodoo to happen?" he asked her.

"Well, I don't really know exactly. All I know is I'm dating someone, and the next thing I know I'm reading his engagement announcement in the newspaper."

Trent was clearly amused. "Let's see, you've lived here three years and made twelve grooms. That's a groom every three months. Quick worker," he said, winking at her playfully.

She frowned at him, but kept her voice low. "I told you I don't 'work' at it. I don't do anything."

He didn't seem to be listening. "Hey, Jim," he called. "How come you didn't tell me my date was a celebrity in town?"

The crowd hushed. "Date?" a few voices gasped, before spontaneous applause broke out. Some of the new grandmothers hugged Maureen, their eyes damp.

Jim looked smug as he strolled up to Trent. "Now, don't tell me I didn't warn you, because when you came through that receiving line and told me you were with Rae, I looked you right in the eye and said that I guessed you were next. Didn't I?"

"Well, yes. But I didn't know what you were—oh, no."

Rae watched Trent's face register a trapped look as realization dawned on him.

Little Ed went over and slapped him on the back. "The man who swore on his classic 1966 convertible that he'd never get married."

"As a math whiz, I can tell you for certain, Trent, that you will be Rae's lucky thirteen," said Mason.

"No, he won't," Rae broke in. If she had to look at the pained expression on Trent's face one more minute, she would be forced to strangle him. "This was a pity date, and that doesn't count. Trent just found me alone in front of the church and was polite enough to offer to escort me. Now, let's all just leave him alone."

"And pass up the chance to put the most avowed bachelor in town to the test?" Jim said. "Not likely."

"You can do it, Rae," added Mason encouragingly.

"I don't do anything!" Rae repeated. "I never did. You all got married because you wanted to. Trent doesn't."

"You're the irresistible force," Little Ed reminded her.

"And he's the immovable object!" said Rae, raising her voice in frustration.

"True. And what possible motivation would she have for trying to budge me?" Trent, who had been listening to the exchange, broke in, trying to lighten the mood. "The last thing she needs is to date a guy like me. It's been called a dead-end street." And the last thing he wanted was to date a woman like her, who was so nice and sweet and . . . irresistible.

Rae jumped back in. "And why would Trent want to date me? I'm sure everyone in town knows by now that what he wants is to get me out of his house so he can sell it. I'm his biggest problem right now."

Little Ed's eyes narrowed thoughtfully. Trent had learned long ago that meant trouble. His redheaded friend might be as big as an ox, but he was also as smart as a whip.

"I think," Little Ed finally drawled, "that is not a problem. It's a solution."

Trent felt the hairs on the back of his neck start to prickle ominously. "What are you talking about, Little Ed?"

"You don't think Rae can turn you into a groom."

"Not her or anyone else on God's green earth."

"Then there's no reason for you to be afraid to let her try," mused Little Ed. "You know...by dating her."

"Wait a minute." Trent held up his hand. "Of course I'm not afraid, but what about Rae? You don't expect me to use her just to prove a point to you?"

Rae put a hand on his arm to stop him. Trent felt threads of pleasure radiating out from her gentle touch. "Just what exactly are you getting at, Little Ed?" she asked.

Little Ed grinned. "I'm thinking that given that Trent here is so sure that he's immune to marriage, it might be fun to raise the stakes this time."

Rae was curious despite herself. "Stakes?"

"The way I see it, all you usually get out of this Groom Maker thing is a few dates with a guy and then an invitation to come watch him marry someone else. But a friendly little bet might make things more interesting. You know, like you bet you can make Trent into a groom and he bets that you can't."

Rae and Trent both opened their mouths to speak, but Little Ed raised his hand. "There'd have to be a time limit, of course," he continued thoughtfully.

"That would be handy. Because if Rae had to date me until I got married, she'd be stuck with me forever," Trent said dryly.

Little Ed ignored him. "Three months is her average, like you said. Wouldn't that make things a little more exciting?"

Rae was shaking her head, but Little Ed went on. "And of course there would have to be a little something on the line."

"Like what?" she asked.

"Something that you both want."

There was a short moment of silence before the faces surrounding Little Ed began to light up, one by one.

"My *house?*" Trent said, incredulous. Little Ed had gotten him to go along with some crazy schemes in his day, but he would have to be certifiably nuts to get roped into this one. Selling that house was crucial to him. "Why in the world would I put that on the line?"

"Why does the immovable object sound so worried?" Mason asked no one in particular.

"You'll never get married, Trent. You've told us so yourself. About a million times," Jim added, straight-faced.

Trent shook his head. "I can't risk the house. When the sale goes through, the buyer will take possession in three months."

"That'll be tough," Little Ed said, "since Rae is supposed to be there for two more years. Unless you're going to break your mother's agreement."

Silence, all around. All eyes were on Rae and Trent, and fleetingly, they met each other's. Could they really do this? By unspoken mutual consent, they stepped apart from the crowd.

"If," Trent said. "If we made this crazy bet, it would replace the agreement you had with my mother."

Rae nodded.

"If I won, I'd want you to move out of the house in three months," he continued.

She nodded again.

"And I suppose if you won, you'd want to stay in the house, rent-free, for two more years."

Rae shook her head. "I'm supposed to do that anyway," she reminded him.

"Then what would you want if you won?"

"I'd want to stay there the two years and then have the option to buy the house from you."

Trent was surprised. "You want to buy the house?"

"More than anything," Rae said. And by then, she'd be able to.

In the silence that followed, Trent thought quickly. If he won—no, *when* he won—he'd have Rae out of the house three months from now, in mid-August, without having to welsh on the agreement his mother had with her. He liked that idea. Then he could go on and sell the house and buy his hotel.

If he lost, he'd have to hang on to the house for two more years, which meant that he'd lose the deal to buy the hotel in Boston. And he'd have to take the option for an additional two years in Tokyo working at his old job. Both unpalatable.

Wait a minute. He had almost forgotten the obvious. Those things weren't even the worst that would happen if he lost the bet. If he lost the bet, he'd be *married.*

Rae felt her disappointment being replaced by hope. Until now, she had fully expected to be packing her bags and her dream up for good. She looked at Trent. If she took the bet and lost, he'd have her out of there, guilt-free. But he was going to have her out anyway; the result would be the same for Rae. She figured it was a long shot that she could make him a groom, but then again, she had nothing to lose by trying. And if she happened to win, her dream would come true. Because not only would she keep her business, she'd be able to buy the house she loved and live in it forever.

"What do you think?" he asked finally.

More silence. "You own the house now. Are you comfortable with the risk?" she asked him.

Trent forced himself to look at the situation objectively. "This is the closest I'll ever come to a sure bet in my lifetime. Like I told you, I will *never* get married." And three months was a short time, he reminded himself. Even people who *wanted* to get married didn't find the right person and have a wedding in three months.

Little Ed approached them. "So what do you say?" he asked Trent. "Are you willing to put your money where your mouth is?"

Trent's decision was made. "I'm willing if Rae is."

"Are you?" Little Ed asked her.

"That depends." Rae regarded Trent closely, then asked Little Ed, "Is he trustworthy?"

Before Little Ed could answer, Trent did. "Absolutely," he said, his gaze unwavering. "I'll stick to whatever we agree on. What are your terms?"

She crossed her arms. "You'd have to cooperate."

"How do I do that?"

"Well, you have to want to date me, and we'd have to see each other regularly. At least three times a week."

Something inside him leapt up at her words; he was ready to jump all over the idea of spending time with Rae, exploring the attraction he felt for her. But something else told him to be wary, because of the kind of woman she was. Not that he thought for a moment that she could actually make a groom out of him. Unless someone was going to put a gun to his head to make him sign a marriage license, he was going to win this bet. "You've done this twelve times before, which means you're the expert. You call the shots. I'm at your command."

Rae ignored his teasing tone and went on seriously. "This is not an exclusive relationship. It's all right to date other people."

Trent put his hands in his pockets, regarding her with what looked like casual interest. "All right, or required?"

Rae frowned. She wanted him to meet his future wife. As soon as possible. But none of the other twelve had actually dated anyone else while they were seeing her. She decided she'd better not push it. "All right," she finally said.

Trent was getting impatient. He knew what he wanted, and he was ready to go for it. "Enough talk," he said, nailing Rae with an inscrutable gaze. "Are you ready for some action?"

Rae didn't take any more time to think. If she did, she was afraid her intellect would pick up on something that her intuition had whiffed on. Some way that she stood to lose on this nothing-to-lose, last-chance, desperation wager. Instead, she looked Trent in the eye and held out her hand. "Grab a tight hold on your bachelorhood, Mr. Colton. You've got yourself a bet."

Chapter Three

News of the bet spread like wildfire through the reception, until ten minutes after Rae had shaken hands with Trent, every man, woman and child in Emerson was intimately acquainted with the details of the wager.

There was no debate about the outcome. Although Trent had the reputation for being notoriously fancy-free and dead set against marrying, well, Rae was Rae. She would make a groom out of him, just as she had with all the others. The only points of debate were who Trent would end up marrying and how soon everyone would be dancing at his wedding.

Maureen sought Trent and Rae out. "Are you sure about this?" she asked Rae.

Rae nodded. "At least this way I have a hope of staying in the house." She didn't relish the thought of playing the groom-making role yet again, but for the sake of the house, she'd do anything. Even that.

Maureen turned to her son. "How about you? You could lose that hotel you want to buy."

"Hell, Mom, I'm grown-up enough to decide whether to risk it on a stupid, immature dare by my buddies," he joked.

Maureen shook her head. "Still, I wish there were some way for you both to get what you want."

"There was no way that could happen," Rae stated. "With this bet, we each have a fighting chance of winning."

"Still, I feel bad that my agreement with you had to be broken," Maureen said to her.

"I take full responsibility for that," Trent reminded his mother.

"This bet is replacing that agreement," Rae added, not wanting the friend who had done so much for her to be upset. "We're both ready to abide by the outcome, aren't we, Trent?"

"Absolutely."

That seemed to satisfy Maureen, who walked off with Trent. Relieved, Rae began to scan the crowd. If she had to get Trent married off in three months, she was not about to miss an opportunity like this. The disc jockey was starting a new set, and if she could get him to dance with an available woman the way he had danced with her earlier, this bet could be over soon.

She zeroed in on a few possibilities just as Trent returned to her side with a piece of the wedding cake, a beautiful multitiered creation baked by Mason's mother. No sooner had they finished eating than Rae found herself being escorted from the reception.

"Don't you want to stay longer?" she asked Trent hopefully. "You only danced with your mother and me. I could introduce you to someone. Or maybe there are some old acquaintances you want to renew?"

He shook his head. "After the flight from Tokyo and two whirlwind days of meetings in Boston, not to mention the day I've spent here, the only acquaintance I want to renew is with my pillow."

In a way, Rae was glad for the excuse to leave. The emotions of the day had exhausted her, too. She could hardly believe that the man walking down Main Street next to her had set foot in town less than twelve hours before.

At the church, he steered her into the parking lot. "I want to get my car," he explained.

"I can walk home from here," Rae offered.

"Hey, I'm not the kind of guy who leaves his women out on the street to walk home alone at night."

Rae turned the idea of being Trent's woman over in her mind. Wait a minute, she reminded herself ruefully. *His women.* How many had there been?

He took her hand. A delicious shiver ran through Rae at the feel of his palm against hers. "I suppose you want this to count as one of our three dates for this week," she teased as he opened the car door for her.

"You're calling the shots."

Rae decided she'd remember that in a few minutes, if a good-night kiss became an issue. If just holding his hand gave her a rush, there was no telling what his kiss would stir up. And one thing was for sure—she had to stay clearheaded so she could concentrate on winning the bet.

At the house, he pulled into the driveway, turned off the engine and walked her to the door. As she fumbled with her key, Rae said, in all honesty, "It was so nice of you to escort me to the wedding, Trent. And I am truly looking forward to going to yours. If you weren't so tired, I'd ask you in, but..."

Her voice trailed off. What in the wide world was she thinking? Ask him in, to his own house? While she stood dumbstruck, Trent fished in his pocket and drew out a key of his own. He unlocked the door and pushed it open, reaching on the inside wall for the switch to turn on the porch light.

"Here you go. I'll call you tomorrow so we can arrange a date," he said. After a moment he gave her a worried look. "Rae? Are you all right?"

"Where are you staying in town?" she asked abruptly.

"At my mother's, for the time being."

For the first time that day, Rae felt truly miserable. "You're doing that because of me, aren't you? Of course you are," she said, answering her own question. "You were planning on staying here in your own house, weren't you?"

"Well, yes," Trent admitted. "Until the lease is up on my condo in Boston, I was going to stay here in Emerson to tie up some loose ends before the sale went through."

Not only that, Rae thought. Now he had to stay in Emerson because of the bet. She let out a sigh.

"Don't worry about it. I'll be perfectly fine at my mother's," he assured her.

Rae looked at him skeptically. Not only was Maureen's house rather small, but she had turned Trent's old bedroom into an office. "Sleeping scrunched up on a lumpy old sofa for three months?" And living with his mother and her husband? Maureen and Hal were dear, but Trent was clearly the independent type.

He grinned good-naturedly. "I'm tough."

Rae made her decision. "No doubt, but in this case there's no reason to be. This house has plenty of bedrooms. I don't see why you and I can't both stay here."

"Wait a minute. You don't have to feel guilty about being in the house. You have every right to be here for the next three months."

"So do you. And I'm not feeling guilty," Rae insisted. "I'm being selfish. Sleeping on that sofa, you'll have the disposition of a grizzly, and then how am I going to get some woman to marry you? You'll be helping my cause if you stay here." She flashed him an encouraging smile.

"People will talk," he warned. "I have a bit of a reputation."

"So I gathered," she said dryly.

"That doesn't bother you?"

She would just have to be on her guard. "I can handle it," she said. "Anyway, I've got a reputation of my own." People wouldn't talk about her if she ran naked down Main Street.

"That's what I mean. You're the Groom Maker, a town legend. Are you sure you want your reputation...ah, besmirched?'' His lips twitched at the corners as he spoke.

Rae rolled her eyes. ''All the more reason for you to stay. My reputation could use a little besmirching.''

Trent hesitated, torn by Rae's unexpected offer. On the one hand, he would be much more comfortable staying here in his own house. But on the other, living under the same roof with Rae would mean daily contact. *Intimate* contact. He didn't know if he should be more worried about whether she would be finding out things about him that she could use to turn him into a groom, or about whether he could manage to keep his hands off her.

''Well, it's your decision, and whatever you decide is fine with me,'' Rae said finally. ''Either way, I'll talk to you tomorrow. Right now, I'm going to bed. Thanks again for tonight.'' She stood on tiptoe and brushed her lips against his cheek.

Her tiny kiss caught Trent off guard, and his reaction to it was even more unsettling. It was immediate, and far from tiny. He wanted to pull her into his arms and give her a real kiss. He wanted to taste her, feel her soft lips on his and hold her closer than he had when they'd danced.

But she had disappeared into the house, leaving him to make his decision.

What decision? Trent thought, as he went to his car and got his suitcase out of the trunk.

The next morning, Trent wondered if he would have slept better if he had gone ahead and kissed Rae the way he'd wanted to.

He had taken the attic bedroom, the one he used to stay in when he spent the night with his grandparents as a kid. Back then, the creaking of the house had kept him awake; last night, his thoughts of the woman sleeping only steps away had allowed him little rest. But now it was morning, and Trent was ready to spend it the way he had always spent Sunday mornings in Emerson.

The house was silent, and he saw no sign of Rae as he left. At the road, he turned and took a good look at the house in the morning light. It was beautifully set up on a little rise, a good distance from the road, and it was the kind of house that made cars going by on the road stop and back up to take a better look. At three stories high, if you included the finished attic, it had been one of the largest houses in town since it had been built more than a hundred years before. Its clapboard sides were painted a pristine white, and it had lots of big windows framed by pairs of black shutters. A wide, wraparound front porch had a swing, and a railing with about a million little spindles Trent remembered painting with his grandfather. There were big window boxes, each filled with a profusion of blossoms, and a garden in the side yard, complete with trellis. The house stood all by itself, surrounded by woods that were part of the property. All was peaceful and still as Trent walked away.

Main Street was quiet, too, with only his footfalls and the birds sounding in the early morning. Then he passed the bakery, and saw Mason's mom inside, getting ready for the morning rush. She waved to him through the window, and Trent felt a shivery sensation of déjà vu. It lingered as he continued walking, and he knew he'd stop back on his way home to buy donuts.

He was probably crazy to think anyone else would be there. It had been a long time since he had been in town on a Sunday morning. It had been a tradition for him and his friends to meet in back of Big Ed's gas station, prop up their feet on a wooden crate and drink soda from those thick-glassed, returnable bottles. If it was football season, they'd talk about the game the day before. When they were old enough, they'd talk about their Saturday-night dates.

And for the first time since Trent had graduated and moved on, he missed those Sunday mornings. It was too much to ask that they could be recaptured now.

But maybe they could. After getting a soda from the machine in front of the station, Trent walked over and saw the old crate in the back. Propped up on it were a pair of long legs that had to be Mason's—hairier than before, but just as skinny. Next to them were Little Ed's unmistakable, freckled tree trunks.

Trent paused. With Jim gone off on his honeymoon, he hadn't expected anyone else to be there. But resting on the crate was another pair of legs. Smooth legs, with beautiful calves curving above slim ankles. Tantalizing legs. Trent knew whose they were. He had seen them before. But not under shorts, which revealed so much more of them.

When he rounded the corner of the garage, it was Rae he looked at, to see her reaction. He wondered what she had been thinking after last night. But though her brown eyes widened for a moment when he appeared, they didn't hint at her thoughts.

"Do we still compare Saturday-night dates here?" Trent asked, sitting down with the others.

"Lucky for you we don't," Little Ed told him. "Can't imagine what horror stories Rae here could tell after having to spend an evening with a seasoned lech like you. But she's too much of a lady to talk anyone down when he's not there."

"I'm here. You can talk me down now," Trent offered to Rae.

"I'll pass," she said, standing up. She bent over both of the baby strollers that were parked nearby and blew kisses into them. Then she got on her bike, which had been leaning against the building. "I'm headed for home. See you guys later."

"I certainly will," Trent said over his shoulder as she pedaled off. His gaze lingered on her until she rode out of sight.

"Why'd she have to go and leave?" Little Ed asked Mason. "Now all we have to look at is his ugly mug."

Mason shrugged. "She didn't seem in much of a hurry until *he* showed up."

"He's going to be hanging around for three months, too." Little Ed continued to address Mason. "I hope she gets him married off fast."

"Good morning to you, too," Trent said, getting back up to peer into the strollers. In each was a tiny occupant, sleeping peacefully. Little Ed's baby, Melissa, was incredibly tiny, with her mother's pert little nose and her own wispy version of her father's flaming hair. Mason's son was older, and a stretch like his dad. He was lying facedown, and the top of his curly blond head and the toes of his blue socks touched the ends of his stroller.

Trent couldn't believe it. He had always thought babies were fascinating. But he had never been able to see their parents in them, until now. Maybe it was because he had been so close to Little Ed and Mason, almost like brothers. Looking at their kids, he could literally see some of the heritage they were passing down to the next generation. Those snoozing kids didn't know it yet, but they were damn lucky to have his buddies for fathers. Trent didn't even have his old man's current address.

"How old were your babies when Michelle stopped breast-feeding?" Little Ed was asking Mason.

"Davey was about eleven months, but she didn't make it that long with this guy," Mason said, nodding toward the stroller. "He kept wanting to tank up every couple of hours, day and night."

Little Ed rolled his eyes in sympathy. "What did she do for sore nipples?" he asked in all seriousness.

Trent had to laugh.

Little Ed rounded on him. "What's so funny?"

Trent propped his feet back on the crate and linked his hands behind his neck. "You guys. Man, have you ever changed. I remember when the only conversations we had about breasts centered on their size. Or the best ways to unhook a bra."

"When your wife is wearing a nursing bra, then we'll talk size and access," Mason said knowingly.

"My wife. Ha."

"The boy just doesn't get it," Little Ed said, shaking his head. "Mason, tell him what he's up against."

"Rae will have you married off so fast you won't remember what it's like to leave the toilet seat up."

"She sure married Jim off fast," Trent said dryly. Jim and Lynna had known each other all their lives, but as far as Trent knew, they had never dated.

"Jim and Lynna were made for each other," said Mason. "But it took Rae to make Jim realize that."

"I take it you went out with her, too?" Trent asked.

"I was number one," Mason said with pride. "If it wasn't for Rae, I wouldn't be the happy man I am today."

Trent took his feet off the crate and leaned in closer, his elbows on his knees. "Tell me, guys. How does she *do* it?"

"She told you last night. She doesn't do anything," Mason said. "She's just . . . Rae."

Little Ed shrugged. "Somehow, being with Rae gets you thinking that the only thing you want to do is settle down, love a woman with your heart and soul, build a home and start a family."

Trent was having a hard time swallowing this. "And you were number . . ."

"Four," Little Ed said. "Yup, that Rae is sure one of a kind. You're a goner, old buddy. But cheer up. Marriage is the best thing that can happen to a man."

"Not to me."

"Especially to you," Mason said with finality.

"Why do you think we needled you into taking that bet?" Little Ed asked. "We just want to see you as happy as we are, old buddy."

"I'm happy single, and I'm going to stay that way."

"Trent, you're going out with the Groom Maker. People who play with fire have a way of getting burned," Mason said with a knowing look.

"This is just the quickest way to get Rae out of my house," Trent said. "And since I'm going to be here awhile, taking care of loose ends, packing things up and selling them off, I might as well be enjoying the companionship of a beautiful woman." A woman who had her work cut out for her, trying to make him husband material. Who would go to lengths to get his cooperation. "It will be an interesting way to pass the time."

Little Ed gave a snort of laughter. Mason just asked, in serious tones, "Where would you like us to have your stag party?"

There was no use arguing with them. But maybe Trent could get some information. "All everyone does is tell me how wonderful Rae is, but twelve men passed up the chance to marry her. You guys are holding out on me. I can feel it. What's wrong with her?"

"Nothing!" Little Ed and Mason blurted out in unison.

"Come on, guys, this is me you're talking to," Trent coaxed.

His friends looked at each other. "We've never really discussed it before," Mason said, hedging.

"Rae really is incredible," Little Ed added. "But..."

Trent tried to keep his tone light. "But what? Look, thanks to you guys, my house is on the line here. I need all the inside information I can get."

Mason relented. "Well, let's just say that the physical part of my relationship with Rae was somewhat...one-sided."

Little Ed nodded. "Mine, too. I think Rae is real attractive, but we never seemed to get anywhere physically, even though I sure wanted to. Rae never really responded to me."

Trent couldn't believe it. He was a man of experience. The dance he had shared with Rae wasn't outwardly erotic, but her sensual response, the feeling of her soft curves gently reshaping against him, had not been his imagination. He would have had to be carved out of wood not to be able to read her body language, not to mention wanting to talk back in that same language. It was the main reason he was glad he hadn't kissed her later on. He couldn't have trusted himself to stop at a kiss. No, there was nothing wrong with Rae in that department.

Had he stumbled onto the secret of the Groom Maker? Maybe, unknowingly, she had submitted those guys to a trial by chastity. After that, they'd married the first woman who said yes. Trent grinned at his friends. "Just because none of you could get her to—"

Faster than a blink, Trent found himself pinned up against the wall of the station by Little Ed's bulk. His huge friend's voice was gruff.

"You were just about to make a serious mistake, my friend. No one talks about Rae like that."

Trent's fight instinct was on full alert, but luckily his intellect was, too. He was not about to call the bluff of a man who outweighed him by tens of pounds, a man he'd seen in action in a few fights, a man who had gotten the drop on him...this time. "All right, buddy," he said softly, trying to make a joke. "No roughing the quarterback, remember?"

Little Ed released him, but his eyes were still hard as flint. "And while we're having this friendly chat, Colton, let me tell you how much I don't like the idea of you living in that house with her."

"Wait a minute. That was her idea. And you all seem to be forgetting that it is *my* house."

Little Ed gave him a low warning. "Let me tell you, if you hurt that woman, I'll hurt you. Bad."

Just then tiny Melissa let out a lusty wail, and Trent watched as the hands that a moment ago had clenched his arms like steel bands gently cradled the helpless infant.

"Feeding time," Little Ed said, and walked away, one-handing the stroller while keeping the baby close to his chest.

Mason got up and started strolling his baby home. "Good luck, Trent. You're going to need it."

As Trent turned the other way, toward his house, he felt a large hand on his shoulder. "You probably don't understand the way we feel about Rae," Little Ed said, from behind him.

On the contrary, Trent had no trouble understanding the protective instincts that Rae called up in Little Ed. She had the same damn effect on him. Otherwise, he wouldn't have let her walk away from him last night.

"No hard feelings?" Little Ed asked.

"Don't act as dumb as you look, big guy," Trent said, with a wry grin.

Little Ed dropped his hand, looking relieved. "See you next Sunday morning?"

"Just try to keep me away."

Trent bought some donuts from Mason's mother on the way back home. The walk gave him time to think about what his friends had said. He could understand perfectly that Rae was not the kind of woman who would fall into bed with every man she went out with. Which made it even more frustrating that he was more attracted to her, in every way, than he'd ever been to a woman. He thought about the dance again, knowing now that she didn't respond like that to just any man.

It was just his luck that she responded to him.

Rae stepped out of the bathroom, hair damp and face flushed from her shower, and smelled coffee brewing. Trent must be back. When she had heard him climb the third-floor stairs last night, she realized that he had gone for the idea of living in the house with her. Now she had to adjust to the reality of it.

He was sitting at the kitchen table, reading the Sunday paper, his bent elbows only serving to enhance the definition of his biceps. He might be a hotel executive, but he didn't get that tan and his rugged build from sitting behind a desk pushing papers all day. She knew he had been quarterback for the high school football team, and she guessed that he was still into sports, and not just as a spectator. He had the economy and grace of movement, the intelligent and watchful readiness—not to mention the competitive-ness—that were the marks of a natural athlete.

And it was all Rae could do not to touch that sandy brown hair with its sun-washed streaks. She wondered if it always looked so deliciously rumpled in the morning. She guessed she would be finding that out.

Realizing that she couldn't hover in the doorway all morning, Rae made herself walk into the kitchen. "Hi," she managed to say.

He looked up from the real-estate page and gave her a smile that made breathing a tad more difficult for her.

"Breakfast's ready," he said, gesturing toward the coffeepot and a box of donuts sitting on the counter.

Rae helped herself and stood leaning against the counter.

Trent looked up again, and pulled out the chair next to his. "Sit," he said.

Rae sat down and smiled to herself, wondering at how he had made the word sound inviting instead of like a command to a pet. She found the sports section and read as she ate. This wasn't so bad, she thought. The less they spoke, the easier it would be to deal with the effect he had on her.

She pretended to herself that she had been relieved that he hadn't returned her good-night kiss, but disappointed was more like it. Deep down, she had hoped that the first man who had ever made her feel a physical spark had felt an answering spark. Even if he wasn't the kind of man she was looking for. With a sigh, she gave up trying to read the paper, and sipped her coffee. When she glanced over at Trent, she found that he was looking at her. He didn't look away. Talk to him, she told herself sternly. Get your infatuation under control and think about your future!

"We need to set up a schedule for seeing each other," she said.

"Schedule?" He sounded surprised. "Is that how you did it with the other guys?"

Rae frowned. "Well, not exactly." She hadn't been trying to make grooms out of the other guys. She had just been dating them because she was interested in them.

"Then how exactly did you do it?"

"There was no formula. We just…saw each other. Sometimes I thought of something to do—sometimes they did."

"Wouldn't it be a little risky to change your methods now?" he asked.

It would be riskier not to go all out to get him married, Rae thought, because what she was risking was her business and her happiness. No, her methods in Trent's case were going to change quite a bit. But she could bend on the schedule.

"Of course, we don't need to schedule our dates for the next three months, or anything like that. But we do need to make sure we have enough time to get together."

Trent smiled. "Rae, I am at your disposal. I will be here for three months, with the exception of occasional trips into Boston, with nothing to do but sell my house, pack up what I want and clear out everything else. When you want to go out, just ask me."

Rae didn't hesitate. After all, she was one of the things he wanted to clear out. "How about Tuesday morning?"

"Tuesday morning? Not exactly prime time for dating."

Rae knew that. She had a plan to carry out, and besides, daylight might cut down on her attraction to him. "Nine-thirty. Can you make it?"

"I can make it. Should we meet at my place or yours?" he asked with a grin.

Rae couldn't help smiling back. "It seems funny to be asking you this, since it's your house, but have you had a chance to see it yet?"

He got up and put his coffee mug in the dishwasher. "I looked around the outside this morning. You've done a great job, Rae. I haven't seen the grounds looking so good since my grandparents lived here."

"Have you looked at the inside?"

"I was just about to. Come with me?"

They started in the room where Rae had set up Styles. Trent had to admit that he was pleasantly surprised. He wasn't sure what he had been expecting when he'd first heard that there was a hair salon in his house. Maybe chrome and bright lights and a row of chairs in a sleek, chic atmosphere. But he found that Rae had been carefully sensitive to preserving the charm of the room, with its big windows and hardwood floors. There was a sink in one corner, and, since she worked alone, just one chair for cutting hair. But the waiting area looked like his grandmother's old sitting room, which it was. Rae had added plants and a few other touches of her own, but all in all, when she moved out there would be little that needed to be done to restore the room to its original state. Trent kept that last thought to himself.

"You've done a good job here," he said simply.

His words meant a lot to Rae. She was proud of Styles, and was glad that her efforts to keep the house as intact as possible hadn't gone unnoticed. She was also a bit relieved. Ever since finding out that Trent hadn't known that she was living and working in his house, she had been afraid he might not approve of what she had done. But that didn't seem to be an issue.

She went along as he walked through the rest of the downstairs rooms. They were neat and clean, quaintly furnished, with just the right degree of well-worn shabbiness to make the place feel homey. Rae had loved the house from the first time she'd seen it. Its only drawback was that it had only the one first-floor bathroom, not too unusual for a house that age. It hadn't mattered when she had lived there alone. But the intimacy of sharing it with Trent had hit her that morning when she'd found his shaving things on the counter.

"When did the house become yours?" she asked him.

"My grandfather died when I was a freshman in college, my grandmother when I was a sophomore. They were my father's parents, and I was their only grandchild. For a number of reasons, they decided to will the house directly to me." One of the reasons was that their only son had left them and Emerson behind after his divorce. Another was that they knew how much Trent had loved the place. "That's when my mother started her boutique here."

They went up to the second floor. "Maureen told me the house is pretty much the way it was when your grandparents lived here," Rae said.

"It is." He opened a door for her, then leaned against it, arms crossed. "Except that someone has invested more than just time in the gardens, and painted some of the rooms. I don't recall seeing bills for any of those expenses," he said, frowning.

"It seemed so little to do, since I was living here for free," Rae said.

"You were taking care of the outside in exchange for rent," Trent responded. "You didn't have to put your own money into the place."

"I love this house. From the moment I saw it, I knew I was meant to stay here," Rae said dreamily.

But you aren't going to, Trent thought, frustrated. He couldn't decide if it would be cruel or kind to say it out loud. One thing was for sure; after seeing how much she loved the place, winning wasn't going to be easy. An unfamiliar ache rose in him.

They moved into the next room, and Rae went over to the window to look down on the garden. She gave a wistful sigh. "I'll bet this old house is just full of memories. I've heard that your grandparents were wonderful people."

Trent came up to stand beside her. "You heard right."

He fell silent, and Rae remembered that his mother had told her that he had spent a lot of time here when he was very young because it was a much happier place than home was. It was no secret in Emerson that Trent's father had been a notorious philanderer. After the divorce, Maureen had done a great job of getting past the pain and getting on with her life. She bore no ill will toward her ex-husband. She had once told Rae that he just never should have married and had a family; he simply wasn't that kind of man.

Rae wondered what it had been like for Trent to have a man like that for a father. Until now, she had never thought about it from the point of view of the boy who was the product of that unhappy marriage. She felt herself warming another dangerous degree toward this man standing next to her, who would be the thirteenth to leave her, whether or not it was to get married.

And he would walk away far more easily than the other twelve, who had gone out with her because they had felt some measure of affection for her. He was dating her only to win the bet, so he could get her out of the house, so he could turn around and sell it. It was clear to Rae that if he was capable of stubbornly selling the house he seemed to be fond of, he would walk away from her without a backward glance.

But this time, she vowed, she wouldn't be left disappointed. This time, she'd be prepared for the leaving.

Chapter Four

On Tuesday morning, it was warm enough to have the top down on Trent's convertible as they drove along the road toward Connecticut.

"Thank you for offering to drive," Rae said.

"My pleasure." Trent found himself enjoying the view. He hadn't been out this way in some time. Besides, he wasn't sure her old car could make it that far.

Rae let her head roll forward so she could massage the stiff muscles at the back of her neck.

Trent glanced from the road. "You all right?"

"I'm fine," Rae said. "I must have just slept on it funny." For the past three nights, she had slept on the couch in her salon. Not the most comfortable way to spend the night, but she didn't feel comfortable going up to the second-floor bedroom she usually slept in, with Trent in the house. They hadn't discussed sleeping arrangements, and as far as Rae was concerned, the less said, the better. She checked the road signs. "Take the next left."

Trent kept his eyes on the road. "How is your business doing?" he asked her.

"It was slow the first year, until I built up a customer base. But things have picked up. I'm busy most of the time."

"You're doing well, then?"

"I'm right on the schedule I set for the business when I started it."

"I take it that having to move out in three months would be a setback for you."

Rae laughed. "If you were your mother, here's the part where I would start lying."

"Why?" Trent looked faintly shocked.

Rae sighed. "I used to work at a big salon. I had a little capital, but no chance for the kind of credit I would need to start my own business, and no connections. After my father died, his old friend Hal Peters introduced me to his wife."

"My mother, the soft touch."

"Exactly. Maureen gave me a break. She claimed that the space in your house was just sitting idle, that you would be away for five years, that having my salon there would bring in business for her boutique, that she would enjoy the company. It was my idea to do the upkeep in lieu of the rent I couldn't pay. And I got more business because of her boutique than she got because of my salon. The truth is, she did it because she was nice. Your mother has a bottomless capacity for sympathy."

Trent's expression was unreadable. "Whereas I am hard-hearted."

"Are you? I don't know you well enough to know that. But I know that because you're a business person, I can answer your question in those terms. When I started this business, I put everything I owned into it. It was a gamble, but a gamble I knew I could win, given the continuation of one circumstance."

"Not paying rent for five years?"

"Bingo."

"Where do you stand now, after three years?"

"Dead even. I've paid off all my debts, including my father's medical bills, and I own my equipment outright, but that's it. In two years, I'll have the down payment for a place of my own," she said. His place.

"You must have other options, if you have to leave now."

Rae shook her head. "There isn't another space in town where I could both live and have my salon, and I simply couldn't afford to pay rent on both a place to live and a place for my business."

"Who says you have to stay in Emerson?"

"I do," Rae said. "For one thing, in a new location I'd have to start from scratch building up a new customer base, which is easier said than done. And as I said, I'm low on capital right now, so low that it may not even be feasible to move my equipment, make modifications to a new space and handle rent payments during that first year or so. But more important, I love Emerson. I feel like I belong there, and I don't want to leave it." She didn't mind his knowing her exact situation. It would be all too clear to the world in a few short months if she lost the bet. She would have to go out of business, and pride had nothing to do with it when her failure would be due to circumstances beyond her control.

"So moving out of my house means you'd have to go back to working for someone else."

Rae couldn't hold back a small sigh. He was too savvy not to guess the truth, though she doubted anyone else in town would. "Yes. And you don't have to be in the hair business to know how huge the gap is, both in money and satisfaction, between being an entrepreneur and being an employee. Take this left."

Trent turned the wheel smoothly. His voice was casual. "You want a job at my hotel?"

Rae laughed. "No. I want you to get married."

"So you can keep your business?"

"And buy your house."

Trent kept his eyes on the road. "The purchase option that you wanted in two years was for real, then."

"Oh, yes. I want that house," Rae said with determination.

It was obvious to Trent how important winning the bet was to Rae. After a few minutes, he said, "Do you know why I'm selling the house, Rae?"

"Yes. You want to use the money to buy your own hotel."

"Like you, I want to be my own boss."

"Like me, you want a place of your own," Rae remarked. "You want your hotel and I want your house. And winning the bet is the ticket there for both of us."

"No, Rae," Trent reminded her in a low voice. "For one of us."

Rae looked out her window. She didn't feel like talking any more. After a while she said, with a cheerfulness she didn't feel, "Here we are."

Trent pulled into a crushed stone driveway. The house at the end of it looked like a gingerbread house, he thought as he pulled in to park next to a school bus. He got out of the car and went around to open Rae's door for her. "What is this place?" he asked.

"A toy museum." She walked toward the building, and Trent fell into step beside her.

"This is your idea of a date?" he said, looking amused.

"It's time spent together, so it counts, city slicker," Rae said with a playful grin. "Dates aren't always dinner and a show, you know. It's amazing where your imagination can take you."

"I know. Right now I'm imagining you threatening me with a popgun until I agree to marry someone."

"Don't tempt me. Especially now that you know how high the stakes are for me."

They went inside, and an attractive young woman behind the reception desk greeted Rae by name. Rae introduced her to Trent.

"Are you giving the tour today, Phoebe?" Rae asked.

The woman nodded and said, "Usual time, so you've got half an hour."

"Come on," Rae said to Trent, grabbing him by the hand. "Let's start on the third floor and work our way down."

The third floor was filled with dolls and doll-houses. To his surprise, Trent found himself looking at the miniature setups with interest.

But he found that even more interesting than the displays was watching Rae looking at everything. Her interest was infectious, and he was sure she was ooh-ing and aahing in her mind. And there was also no doubt that his attraction to her was growing with each moment he spent with her, no matter where they were. He was going to have to do something about it, he told himself. What he was going to do, though, was a bit unclear. He knew exactly what he'd do under normal circumstances. But the situation he was in with Rae was unusual, in more ways than one.

He stepped up behind her, close. "You're really into this, aren't you?" he said. Her obvious pleasure re-minded him of the time she had walked barefoot across the town green.

They were on the second floor and Rae was look-ing dreamily down at an intricate model of a merry-go-round made of tin. "Mmm," she murmured. "His-tory is one of my passions."

Trent filed that one away for the future. Any infor-mation he could get on her just might help him win the bet. "They just announced a tour starting in five minutes. Is that part of our date?"

"Oh, yes, the tour..." Rae's voice trailed off as something in a nearby display case of wooden toys captured her attention. But Trent managed to tear her away from that and one filled with mechanized banks in time for the beginning of the tour guide's talk.

The tour was very thorough, and Trent had to admit that it was fascinating. No wonder Rae seemed enthralled, even though it could hardly have been her first visit there, since she was on a first-name basis with the tour guide. At the end of the tour, Phoebe came over to talk to her and Trent. When he asked her a question about the train display in the next room, the guide led him there to show him something relevant to the answer. Rae slipped quietly to the other end of the first floor, which had been darkened to show a film of early cartoons.

She couldn't have planned it any better, she thought, glancing back through the doorway at Trent, who stood with his back toward her, nodding at something Phoebe said. In the dim light, Rae closed her eyes and leaned her shoulder against the wall, reaching back to rub her stiff neck. Her awareness of time and place faded as she listened to the music and narration. But she snapped back to the present when she sensed that Trent had returned. She was as aware of his presence close behind her as if it had been full daylight and he had been standing right in front of her.

Then, incredibly, she felt his hands start to massage her neck. It felt wonderful. She stood there in the semidarkness, her back still to him, feeling all her tension and soreness disappear under the warmth of his strong yet gentle fingers.

His voice came soft and low. "You wouldn't get a stiff neck like this if you slept on one of the beds instead of on the couch in your salon."

"I didn't know you've been doing bed checks," she murmured.

"Given that you invited me to stay at the house with you so I wouldn't have to sleep on a couch, it seems silly for you to do it," he said. "If you're worried that I'll attack you in your sleep, let me assure you that's not my style."

Instinctively, she knew he was right. A man who looked the way he did, and exuded charm the way he did, was not a man who would be wanting for bed partners. All he had to do was use his hands as he was right now, and most women would be putty in them. Before she became just that, Rae spoke.

"Did you and Phoebe have a nice talk?"

"Yeah. She sure knows a lot about toy trains." His hands continued working their magic.

Darn! Rae thought. Were they talking toys the whole time? "If there's anything else you'd like to talk to her about, go right ahead. Don't worry about me."

Trent's hands dropped from her neck. "Rae," he said. He put his arms around her, linking his hands across the front of her in a loose embrace. She felt his breath, warm against her ear, as he whispered, "I know what you're trying to do."

"What?" Rae must have stiffened involuntarily, because she felt his arms tighten almost imperceptibly around her.

"Don't play innocent. I know when I've been set up."

She gave up all pretense. "Did it work?" she asked eagerly.

Trent gave a low chuckle. "Work? It might have been a little embarrassing for the two of us, but luckily your friend caught on to your trick as quickly as I did. She said to tell you that she's happily dating a schoolteacher from Auburn who brought his class through a few weeks ago.''

''Darn.'' Phoebe was smart and fun and pretty and nice, and Rae was sure Trent would have fallen for her, if someone else hadn't gotten there first.

Trent dropped his voice even lower. ''Just so we don't have any more misunderstandings like this one, let me tell you something. There's only one woman I'm interested in right now and for the next three months. Do you know who that is, Rae?''

She had a pretty good idea what he was going to say, but she shook her head, not trusting herself to speak. It was impossible not to be highly aware of his chest against her back, his hard thighs brushing against the curve of her derriere.

''You are the one.''

His voice was a rumble in her ear, and an echoing shiver vibrated through every nerve ending in her body.

He meant, of course, because she was the woman he had to get out of his house. ''I'm certainly the one making life complicated for you right now,'' she said, trying hard to make her words sound light.

''That's one way to put it.'' Trent gave her a final squeeze and backed away, feeling a sudden determination that she have no idea just how complicated she was making his life. In that position, she would have figured it out before long.

''You're not exactly making my life a bed of roses,'' Rae countered, as she turned to face him. ''If you won't even consider dating a woman, how am I supposed to get you married off?''

"You're not," Trent said with a half grin. "That's the whole point."

"Just watch me," Rae said. She reminded herself that although the bet might be a game to him, it was dead serious for her. She *had* to get someone to marry him. "Are you free on Thursday night?" she asked casually as they walked over to look at a grouping of miniature knights in front of a tiny castle.

"For you, fair damsel in distress, anytime," he said, with a mock bow. "This knight awaits your bidding."

Damsel she was—in distress she was not. At least not until she lost the bet. "Thursday it is," she said. "But don't for a minute think you have me fooled with that fake chivalry act. You are definitely not the kind of knight all those romantic tales have been written about." Then she looked at her watch. "Styles opens in one hour. Are you ready to go?"

If he had said no, Trent was sure she would have walked. Rae was one determined woman.

But then again, he was determined, too. And ready to foil any other schemes to marry him off that she might dream up.

Over the next couple of days Trent found out a lot more about Rae, and everything confirmed his first impression of her. As far as he could tell, she was what everyone in Emerson didn't hesitate to tell him any chance they got—kind, free-spirited and a paragon of virtue.

It wasn't just what other people were saying, either. After all, he and Rae were living in close contact. Very close. Close enough that he heard her soft sighs while she slept at night in the room at the bottom of the stairwell from his. Close enough to see her warm smile a dozen times a day, to smell her earthy rich perfume when she came in from working in the garden, to hear the music of her laughter, to feel her sweet friendship.

She honestly liked him. Him, the man who was going to throw her out onto the street and ruin her business and her dreams. He might be in the right, but that didn't stop Trent from experiencing a feeling that was awfully close to guilt. But then he would remind himself that not only had she agreed to the bet, but she had also been given fair warning that she couldn't possibly win.

And truth was, he liked her, too. He liked the way she sang loud and cheerful and off-key in the shower, and used all the hot water, and then when he said something about it, chided him for the low water pressure as if she were a real paying tenant. He liked the way her soft hands held his when she took out a splinter for him, and the way she woke up all dreamy eyed and fuzzy around the edges.

And he didn't want to think about why he left notes on the kitchen table telling her where he had gone and when he'd be back. Or why he picked up her grocery list when he left to do errands. Or why he was having such a hard time sleeping lately.

So he didn't. It was Thursday, and he had other things on his mind. Like spending the evening with Rae for their second date.

Of course, after their first date, he was ready for anything. Even a date that was going to start at Big Ed's service station, where Rae had asked him to meet her in the note she had left him on the kitchen table. Chuckling to himself, Trent walked out the door.

"Are you sure she'll be here?" Rae asked Little Ed. Her voice held a slight tremor. She was counting on everything going just right tonight.

"Positive. She comes in for a fill-up and oil check every Thursday night after work, six-thirty on the dot."

"Great." Rae relaxed a bit. "Now remember, all you have to do is introduce them. No pushing, no winking. Just introduce. If Trent doesn't leave with her, tell him to meet me at the bank."

Little Ed shook his head. "I don't know what you've got planned, Rae, but if you're trying to pull something over on old Trent, I wish you luck. Let me tell you, when it came to locker-room pranks, he was always one step ahead of everyone else."

Rae laughed. "I'll be sure to remember that if I ever feel the urge to snap a towel at him. This is important, Little Ed! Thanks for your help." She got on her bike and pedaled down Main Street to the bank.

At the bank, she made sure she got the teller with the gorgeous black hair and the sea green eyes. Handing her a withdrawal slip, Rae said, "Hi, Janelle. Would you do me a favor?"

"A mere favor, for the woman who rescued me from the frizzies? I'd give you the keys to my new car if you asked."

Rae laughed. "Nothing that drastic. Do you know Maureen's son, Trent?"

Janelle smiled, counting out Rae's money. "Who doesn't know, and want to grab, the biggest hunk in town? Your hunk, I believe?"

Rae stuffed the money into an envelope. "Yes. No! I mean yes, he is the biggest hunk in town, but no, he's not mine. He's up for grabs."

"You mean you're really trying to marry him off?"

"I sure am. I have to win that bet," Rae said. "He's going to come in here tonight. Would you give him this envelope?"

"No problem, Rae. Is he really free for the grabbing?"

"Absolutely. Give it your best shot. But if he gets away, and wants to know where I am, send him next door to the library."

It was the same at the library, then across the street at the package store, Mason's mother's bakery, the variety store and the apothecary. Rae couldn't believe her good luck. Everyone she had thought would be working that night was, and all were happy to do a small favor for her. As she pedaled home, Rae thought ruefully of how many favors she owed now. But the plan had fallen into place so nicely. She didn't expect to see Trent for a while, or maybe at all that night. If she was really lucky, she told herself.

It was such a warm evening that she poured herself a glass of iced tea and brought it out onto the porch.

Settling onto the old porch swing, she started it rocking. The creaking of its ancient chains must have lulled her into a doze, because the next thing she knew, she felt the swing shift and adjust to a new weight that settled down next to her. Her eyes flew open. It was Trent, with a paper bag in his hand and a grin on his face.

"I've had a very interesting evening," he said, putting the paper bag down on the porch floor. "Warm, isn't it?"

Rae handed him her iced tea. Watching him take a long drink from her glass, she felt a thrill of intimacy.

"Ah. That's better. Now, as I was saying, I think this second date of yours has outdone the first. Want to hear about my evening?"

Rae gave a thin smile. "Sure."

He put his arm across the back of the swing, behind Rae. "Well, first off, let me tell you how much I was anticipating this evening. I knew I was in trouble when instead of finding you at Big Ed's, all I see is Little Ed with a silly grin on his face. I ask him where you are, and he holds me up for ten minutes, telling me about how loud Melissa can belch after her feedings, when all of a sudden this woman drives in for a fill-up. Little Ed just *has* to introduce me to this woman."

Rae couldn't help interrupting. "What was she like?"

"She was all right."

"All right?" Rae blurted out. Candi was not "all right." She was drop-dead gorgeous. Rae knew, because she cut her hair.

Trent looked at her in amusement. "Anyway, finally Little Ed tells me to meet you at the bank. Where Janelle gives me a come-on smile and an envelope of your money, and finally sends me to the library."

"You know Janelle?"

"We went through school together. She was the first girl in our class to wear makeup. I think she wears contact lenses to get her eyes that color."

"She's really nice," Rae said staunchly.

"Agreed. So is her twin sister, Janet, who was working at the library tonight. She handed me this video and sent me across the street to the package store."

He pulled the video out of the bag. "This was my favorite movie when I was a kid," he said, looking at Rae. "Such a coincidence that with all the current movies the library has, this would be the one you check out tonight."

Rae shrugged, trying to look innocent. Then he put a cold six-pack of root beer on her lap.

"Also my favorite, before I discovered real beer. Rita had it all ready and waiting at the counter of the package store." He opened up a can and took a swig, then handed it to Rae.

Rae put the other five cans on the floor of the porch, then took a drink. "It's good," she said, looking up at him. "And that Rita is a sweetheart."

"Sure is. She sent me next door to the bakery, where Mason's cousin Carleen handed me these fresh-baked bulkie rolls." He dropped them in her lap, along with another package. "And sent me along to Jane at the variety store, who gave me some sliced porketta."

"Looks delicious," Rae said, piling the spicy meat onto the rolls. She handed one of the sandwiches to Trent, who took a bite.

"Aren't many places in the world you can get a porketta sandwich," he said with a sigh.

Rae ate hers, too. When she finished, she saw that Trent was looking at her, smiling, but not saying anything. She couldn't stand it any longer. "Then what?"

"Then this." He handed her a cup with a lid on. "Next door at the apothecary, Wanda behind the soda counter gave me this chocolate frappé." He unwrapped a straw he fished from the bottom of the bag and popped it in, then held the cup up to Rae. She took a long pull on the straw.

"Mmm." Rae closed her eyes. The thick, New England-style milkshake was good, but not nearly as delicious as the feeling that had suddenly come over her as she sat side by side with this man, who had his arm resting along her shoulders now, who was smiling at her, swinging with her, holding the cup for her. He spoke to all of her senses at once, and at that moment, the last thing on her mind was handing him over to someone else.

He took a drink of the frappé, then started chuckling.

"What's so funny?" Rae asked.

"What's so funny? You send me out on a wild-goose chase, practically throwing me at the feet of every available woman in this town, and you ask me what's so funny?" Trent wiped the corners of his eyes, then tipped Rae's chin up so that she had to look at him. "I think the matchmaker has finally met her match."

"That's not matchmaking," Rae countered, defending herself. "That's giving you an opportunity to see what's available out there."

Trent ignored her. "You know, if you want to play matchmaker, you could hardly have a better setup than here, cutting the hair of every woman in town right under my nose."

"I don't want to play matchmaker! But you're being so stubborn. I'm just trying to give myself an even chance."

"Who's being stubborn?" To Rae's annoyance, Trent still looked amused. "I believe I told you very clearly that trying to fix me up with other women wouldn't work."

"I just haven't found the right woman yet, that's all," Rae said resolutely.

"And you won't," Trent assured her. "Didn't I tell you that you're the one I'm interested in?"

Rae rolled her eyes.

"Anyway, thanks for all the trouble you went to to find out my favorite things." He gathered up the remains of their dinner and opened the door. "C'mon," he said with a grin and a wink. "This date's not over yet. We've got a movie to watch."

When Trent woke up early on Saturday morning, he immediately thought of Rae. He wondered if she was awake. One of the things he had found out while living with her was that she was an early riser. He was, too. Now.

His attraction to Rae had grown, not fizzled out, as he'd hoped, despite the fact that he had still not allowed himself to so much as kiss her. What Rae had aroused in him was strong enough to have propelled him into more early-morning runs and late-night cold showers than he cared to think about.

But she was exactly the kind of woman he couldn't allow himself to get involved with. She was sweet and wholesome and pure, and a man like him would break her heart into pieces. He was always careful to choose women who knew exactly what they were getting into with him, and wanted it. Rae couldn't be less like that kind of woman.

Yet, he was attracted to her, and he couldn't get away from that. Or from the fact that he was committed to being with her for three months.

Still, it might have been easier to handle his attraction to her if it hadn't been for her attraction to him. He could feel it when he brushed against her, could see it shining out through her eyes when she looked at him. It was as compelling as it was dangerous.

He sat up in bed, stretching, and looked out of his third-floor window. Down below, he saw her. She was kneeling in the garden, barefoot, a shaft of early sunlight lending radiance to her long white nightgown. An angel in his backyard.

Once again, Trent felt drawn to her on some elemental level. He pulled on a pair of sweatpants and went outside.

Watch your step, Trent Colton, he cautioned himself as he walked barefoot across the grass. After all, this was no ordinary woman he was dealing with. This was Rae, and he found her utterly enchanting.

He approached quietly, not wanting to disturb her. She was leaning forward, eyes closed, a soft smile on her lips. Her hands were buried to the wrist in a mound of freshly turned soil.

"Hello." She greeted him with the warmth of welcome in her voice, though she neither turned around nor opened her eyes.

Most people would have been embarrassed at being caught like that, but not Rae. Trent stood next to her, unable to take his eyes from the beautiful picture she made.

Rae took a deep breath that he could almost feel in his own lungs. And without her asking, and without his thinking about it, he knelt down next to her and buried his own hands in the rich brown earth.

It felt surprisingly warm, and welcoming. It had been a long time since the days that he had worked this same soil. He spread his fingers, closed his eyes and gave himself up to the sensation.

"Can you feel it?" Rae breathed.

Trent felt. He spread his fingers and then clenched them into fists of dirt. He felt as if he wanted to grab hold of it somehow.

"It's time," Rae said, finally opening her eyes to meet his. "Time for roots to stretch and grow and take a firm, healthy hold."

She was talking about plants, Trent reminded himself. Just the way his grandfather used to talk in late May. Her words held no message for a man who had left his roots and who was consciously choosing not to put down new ones.

Rae stood up and stretched, breaking the spell, spreading her arms wide in the sunshine. "Time to stop playing in the dirt," she said, laughing and reaching down a soil-covered hand to him. "Are you free tomorrow?"

Trent stood up, brushing crumbs of dirt from his palms. "Uh-oh. What kind of date do you have lined up this time?"

"Actually, I'm putting you to work before I marry you off," Rae said, dimples flashing. "It's time to plant our garden."

Chapter Five

Our garden. Trent figured those two words had crossed his mind about a hundred times since early morning, when Rae had spoken them so easily.

It didn't really mean anything, he told himself. It just made sense. They were living in the house together, and would be for the next three months. They might as well be eating fresh vegetables.

Rae had told him that Saturday was a busy day for her in the salon, so he decided to stay out of the way of her and her customers by tackling one of the outdoor jobs he had to do before he sold the house. He would start on the large shed out back where the driveway ended, which served as a garage as well as a storage area. He'd have to go through it to see what should be thrown away, what he would keep and what he would try to sell. Easier said than done, given that

THE EDITOR'S "THANK YOU" FREE GIFTS INCLUDE:

▶ Four BRAND-NEW romance novels
▶ A Porcelain Trinket Box

PLACE
FREE GIFT
SEAL
HERE

YES! I have placed my Editor's "thank you" seal in the space provided above. Please send me 4 free books and a Porcelain Trinket Box. I understand I am under no obligation to purchase any books, as explained on the back and on the opposite page.

215 CIS AWJD (U-SIL-R-09/95)

NAME

ADDRESS   APT.

CITY   STATE   ZIP

Thank you!

DETACH AND MAIL CARD TODAY!

THE SILHOUETTE READER SERVICE™: HERE'S HOW IT WORKS

Accepting free books places you under no obligation to buy anything. You may keep the books and gift and return the shipping statement marked "cancel". If you do not cancel, about a month later we will send you 6 additional novels, and bill you just $2.44 each plus 25¢ delivery and applicable sales tax, if any.* That's the complete price, and—compared to cover prices of $2.99 each—quite a bargain! You may cancel at any time, but if you choose to continue, every month we'll send you 6 more books, which you may either purchase at the discount price...or return at our expense and cancel your subscription.

*Terms and prices subject to change without notice. Sales tax applicable in N.Y.

the shed was full to overflowing. His grandfather had been a pack rat, and Trent had thrown some of his own things in there, as well. It would be a full day's job and then some.

Besides, if he kept busy, maybe he wouldn't think so much about gardens. Or roots.

Rae watched from the kitchen window as Trent started work in the shed, munching on a bagel before she opened Styles for the day. It was plain to see that he was getting the place ready for the sale. Much as Rae wanted to see that shed put to order, the reason behind it was depressing.

Here it was, a week after they had made the bet, and she was no closer to getting Trent married off than she had been when they had first shaken hands on it. And no closer to being able to stay here in the house. She told herself to start thinking of a new plan, but found she was putting much more thought into how good Trent looked in a work shirt and a pair of old jeans.

With a sigh, Rae admitted to herself that her feelings about Trent—or rather, her feelings *for* Trent— were becoming all too clear. Her fascination with him burgeoned. He crowded into her thoughts, knocking the rational side of her off-balance. He eased into her fantasies, sending the emotional side of her soaring.

She thought about that morning. When he had found her in the garden, he hadn't laughed, or teased, or questioned her, as most people would have. He just listened.

It felt good, that unquestioned acceptance. Maybe that was why, when he had knelt down next to her, she had felt a spiritual bond with him. She wondered if he had felt it.

Gosh sakes, she scolded herself a split second later. She was really reading into things now. And that was sure to be a mistake, given all that she had heard about him.

She heard more later that day when a number of women who had gone to high school with Trent were in the salon at the same time.

"Good luck, Rae," one of them said. "You've got your work cut out for you."

"So I hear."

"No, really. We all grew up in Emerson. And we know Trent is the last man on earth who would ever get married."

Rae kept her eyes on her cutting. "I gather he made a reputation for himself here as some kind of ladies' man."

They all laughed. "That's an understatement," another said. "Did you know that he dated every girl in school?"

Rae's scissors stopped. "Every girl?" It had to be an exaggeration.

"Every single girl, including all of us. And let me tell you, I for one will never forget the good-night kiss he gave me on my parents' front porch."

The third one fanned herself. "That boy was some kisser back then. I'll bet he's even better at it now, after all that practice."

"I'll bet he's good at *everything* now," said the first, with a meaningful lift of one eyebrow.

Rae was still thinking about that conversation when she ran into Trent in the kitchen after she'd closed up for the day. There were a couple of sandwiches on the counter, and he was pouring himself a glass of iced tea, which he handed over to her. Rae saw that the pitcher was empty, so she handed the glass right back to him. If she had learned one thing about him during the week, it was that he loved her homemade iced tea. She put some water on to boil for the next batch and got herself a soda.

"Thanks," he said, taking a long swig. He gave one of the sandwiches to Rae and they sat down at the table, eating. "How was your day?" he asked.

It was such a simple question, but so nice to hear. "Busy, but I like them that way. How was yours?"

"Mine was busy, too. I spent it throwing rusty old car parts and other junk into the back of Little Ed's pickup truck. I think half the dirt in Emerson was living in that shed," he said. "Kind of makes you wonder why just about every customer who came out of your salon came out back there to talk with me."

"Really?" Rae sat up straighter. "How did it go?"

"Great, for me. I didn't propose to any of them." He took a bite of his sandwich.

"You could at least look a little upset about that, for my sake," Rae grumbled, slumping down in her chair.

"Sorry to put you to all that trouble for nothing," he teased.

"Trent Colton, I did not send those women out there," she countered. "Then again, if I had thought of it..."

Trent grinned. "Maybe some of them are trying to cash in on the odds. You are aware of the side betting going on in town?"

Rae nodded, feeling her cheeks grow warm. She had been told that it was the hottest game in town, surpassing both the state lottery and the church bingo. "How are the odds running?"

"Three to one says you'll get me to the altar."

Rae gulped down the last bite of her sandwich. "Not if you don't alter your attitude and start giving some of these women serious consideration," she said, heading out the door so that she wouldn't have to hear him chuckling.

He caught up with her in the driveway. "Where are you going in such a hurry?"

"The nursery closes in less than an hour. I've got to get the things we need for tomorrow," Rae said as she opened her car door.

"Let's take the truck," he said. "We'll swing by the town dump and get rid of this junk, then we can put the flats in the back of it."

"All right." Rae had to admit that she was glad to have Trent's company, as much as his help. She was dog tired from being on her feet all day, and imagined he must feel the same. She stretched and sank down into the battered seat as he drove off. "Nice of Little Ed to let you use his truck."

"Nice? He got the better end of the deal. I swapped him the use of my sports car," Trent said ruefully.

"I'm sure he'll take care of your baby," Rae teased. "You really love that car, don't you?"

"I fixed it up myself, with my grandfather, right in that shed I've been cleaning up all day."

The wistful note in his voice did not go unnoticed by Rae, who decided it would be wise to refrain from comment.

The trip to the nursery was actually fun. It was an old-time place on the opposite edge of town that didn't presume to call itself a "garden center." But they found everything they needed. Trent was agreeable to her plans, which meant all the more to Rae given that he was also knowledgeable about gardening. He must have done a bit of work in his grandparents' garden. She liked the suggestions he made about a few things to plant that she hadn't in the years she had lived in the house.

While he was busy loading the flats into the pickup truck, Rae went to pay.

"What's this I hear about a bet?" Grace, who ran the nursery with her husband, was one of the first people Rae had met when she'd moved to Emerson.

Rae told her the details.

"That's crazy!" Grace said when Rae had finished.

"I know. When I stop to think about it, I can't believe I'm doing it." She used to have such a normal life, Rae thought with a sigh.

"That's not what I mean. I mean, Trent's crazy to think he could win!" Grace said.

Rae rolled her eyes.

Grace touched her on the arm. "Say, who's that he's with, Rae?"

Rae looked over to see Trent release a woman from a hug, then lean back against the truck to talk to her. She was cute and bubbly and gesturing enthusiastically with her hands. "I don't know. I've never seen her before."

"Well, you're the expert," Grace said, handing Rae her change. "But I'd say that there's a prospect he seems to be showing interest in. Come on, Rae. I'm gonna put some money on you. Go for it!"

Rae walked slowly over to the truck. Trent wasn't just making polite talk with this woman. He seemed genuinely interested in her.

"Oh, Rae, there you are. Do you know Gina?" he asked when he saw her.

"No. Hi, I'm Rae."

"Hi." The woman—*young* woman—smiled at Trent. "Are you two..."

"Planting a garden?" Trent said. "How did you guess?"

He might have finished the sentence the way Gina was going to, Rae thought. It wouldn't have killed him to have said they were *dating*.

"It's just so good to see you again, Trent!" Gina gushed.

"You, too."

She grabbed his hand. "Are you free tonight? Right now?"

"Gina, look at me!" Trent said with an easy laugh, holding his arms out from his sides.

Rae tapped her foot. He hadn't been worried about his appearance earlier, when he'd claimed that hordes of freshly coiffed women were stalking him in the shed.

Gina dismissed that with a wave of her hand. "You aren't going to stand on ceremony with me, are you, Trent Colton? I've seen you looking a lot worse than that."

Apparently they knew each other quite well, Rae thought. She cleared her throat. "Trent, I..."

"C'mon, Trent," Gina coaxed. "It'll be fun."

Trent turned to Rae. "You don't mind driving the truck back, do you, Rae? I'll unload it tomorrow, of course."

Rae couldn't believe it. He was going to go. He was actually interested in this woman, who was perky as a cheerleader and not a whole heck of a lot older. To her chagrin, Rae found that she was dismayed instead of overjoyed, as she should have been. "How will you get back?" she asked.

"I'll take him wherever he wants," Gina offered happily.

I just bet you will, Rae thought, climbing into the driver's seat. It took all she could do to smile sweetly out of the open window and say, "Nice to meet you, Gina."

She didn't say anything to Trent, but growled under her breath as she started the engine. Things were getting too complicated. Now she wondered whether she was more worried about losing the bet or losing Trent.

Thump! As she started to pull away, Trent jumped onto the running board next to her. Rae stepped on the brakes. "Change your mind?" she asked.

"Oh, no. Don't worry about that. I know how disappointed you would be if I didn't go with her. I just realized that you paid for this stuff, and I wanted to pay you back."

Disappointed. Right. "You're a big boy, Trent," Rae said, taking the bills he handed her. "You go with whomever you like."

He grinned at her. "Hey, you don't have to pretend with me. I know you must be thrilled at the prospect of leaving me alone with a woman."

Rae looked around the cab of the truck, but there was nothing she could hit him with that would make a dent in his thick skull. "Yes, thrilled. Now, you two kids get going. Don't keep her waiting on my account."

A teasing smile came to Trent's lips. "Do my ears deceive me, or do I detect a hint of hostility in your voice?"

"Why should I feel hostile toward the one woman you are finally showing interest in?" Rae countered, aware that her jaw was tight with tension. "This is not hostility—this is delight."

"That's why I feel guilty," Trent said, his smile turning sheepish. "It was fun to tease you, but I know what you're thinking."

Rae sincerely hoped not. All she needed was for him to suspect that she was interested in him herself.

Trent went on. "It just doesn't seem fair to let you go away with your hopes up about winning the bet."

"You haven't even left the parking lot, and you're telling me you're not going to marry her?" Rae asked. "You can't possibly know that."

"Yes, I can." His teasing grin was back.

"How?"

"Gina's my cousin."

Rae reached out the window to strangle him, but Trent was too quick. He jumped off the running board and disappeared into his cousin's car.

The next day, Rae was already at work in the garden when Trent came back from his Sunday-morning get-together with the guys. He joined her, and they worked steadily through the morning.

"I really had you going last night, didn't I?" he ventured when they were working side by side with spades, turning over the soil.

Rae stabbed at the earth. "Sure did," she answered. He didn't have to know that what he had gotten her going on wasn't hopes of winning the bet, but jealousy, pure and simple. Over his cousin, for gosh sakes. She felt like the village idiot.

Trent stuck his spade into the ground and wiped his brow with the back of his hand. Rae stopped working, too, and rested her hands on the top of her spade. "Did you have a good time?"

"Yeah. We went to Gina's house—actually, her parents' house. She just graduated from U Mass and is living with her folks. They were just putting dinner on the grill, so I joined them."

"It must be great to have family you can visit like that."

"Don't you?"

Rae shook her head. "My parents were both only children, and my mother died the year before my father did. I think I have some distant relatives scattered around the country, but none nearby enough to make a difference," she said. "Are Gina and her parents from your father's side of the family?"

Rae noticed the way Trent clenched his jaw when she mentioned his father. He nodded, then picked up his spade and started digging again. After a few minutes, he turned over a rock, picked it up and tossed it onto the grass. "Listen, Rae. Don't ever get your hopes up again about my getting married. To anyone. It's just not going to happen."

Rae pushed back the wisps of hair that had come loose from her braid. "If it'll make you feel better, I promise I won't get my hopes up about marrying you off." A promise that was only getting easier to keep, for more than one reason.

After lunch, they were ready to start the actual planting. They decided what would go where and divided up the duties. Trent planted the seed packets while Rae put in tiny seedlings. When they were both finished, they did the tomatoes together. They had agreed to put in lots of them because they gave a high yield with a minimum of fuss, and Rae wanted to donate the extras to a food pantry. They worked more slowly now, under the late-afternoon sun, one row apart.

Rae was feeling giddy, staring at Trent's back. She giggled out loud.

He turned around. "What's so funny?"

"I was just thinking how we look about as good as some of the slugs we dug up today."

He grinned, wiping a swath of dirt across his cheek with the back of his hand. "Speak for yourself. Me, I'm as fresh as . . ."

"That pile of nature's fertilizer over by the shed," Rae said, finishing the thought.

"I don't know how you got a reputation for being so nice. You're sure nasty to me."

"Oh, the people in town just see one side of me," Rae said resignedly. "And if you ask me, they don't know you very well, either."

"What do you mean?"

"I don't know how you got such a nasty reputation."

"Hey, I worked hard to build that reputation, so watch it. One good word from you, and all that work gets blown out the window."

"I can see why you'd want to protect your image. Rumor has it you're a great kisser," Rae teased.

"That's not a rumor. It's the truth," he said, bobbing his eyebrows at her. "Come on over to my row, and I'll prove it."

"Given your current resemblance to one of the less palatable varieties of garden vermin, I'll pass."

He laughed. "Your loss."

Rae patted the loose earth around the cherry-tomato plant she had just planted. "Did you really date every girl in town when you were in school?"

"Do you really need to know that?"

"Oh, yes," she said, plastering a serious expression on her face. "For the bet."

"Oh, well, in that case. Yeah, I did," he said. Rae looked at him in undisguised wonder.

"But only once each," he added quickly.

"Was it some kind of dare by your friends, like our bet?" It seemed a rather odd thing for a boy to do.

"No. I just liked to play the field. Still do. I'm telling you, Rae, I am the ultimate bachelor."

Rae made a hole for the next plant. She wondered if his bachelor status had something to do with his parents' divorce. If he only went out with each girl one time, he could never hurt any of them the way his father had hurt his mother.

Trent planted the last tomato bush, stood up and brushed the dirt off his hands. "I'll bet you wish you never made that bet now," he said, trying to joke.

"True," Rae answered honestly. She wished she hadn't had to make it. That he didn't have to be so dead set against marriage.

She decided right then and there that it was time for a new strategy. She had never liked playing the matchmaker, and now that she knew it wouldn't work, she could give up that role for good. Instead, she'd try her hand at nurturing the growth of Trent's roots.

Because only a person who was firmly grounded could take risks. And no matter what he said, she had a suspicion that for Trent, marriage was the biggest risk of all.

Rae made sure she kept Trent in Emerson for their dates that week. One night they went to the pizzeria where Trent and his friends had hung out in high school. Instead of arranging for eligible women to be nearby, Rae asked Mason and Little Ed and their families to join them.

On Friday night they went to the town's old movie theater—a gorgeous relic that showed second-run movies, but packed 'em in anyway. They sat in the balcony and shared an armrest and a carton of popcorn.

Rae didn't know if Trent possessed incredible restraint or if she possessed an incredible imagination. She *thought* he was attracted to her. But he never made a move. Then again, maybe she was wrong. After all, he saw her at her worst, living here in the house. He saw her first thing in the morning, and dead tired after working all day.

He would see her that way again today. As on most Saturdays, her schedule was full to the brim, and seeing Trent in the next room while she was trying to cut hair kept her grasping for the fine edge of her concentration.

Compounding her frustration was what Trent was doing in the next room. He was helping his mother close up her business.

Between customers, Rae stepped through the doorway between Styles and the boutique. She and Maureen had always left the door open so customers could browse and so Rae could get to the phone that they shared. Now the phone was about the only thing left in the room.

Rae watched as Trent muscled a box onto his shoulder and disappeared out the other door. Alone, she and Maureen looked at each other.

Rae's voice echoed in the empty room. "Now that the time has come, I can't believe you're really leaving."

"Not leaving, Rae. I'll still be living right in this town."

"Yes, but you won't be right in the next room."

Maureen turned a slow circle in the center of the room. "This has meant a lot to me."

Rae swallowed. "You seem so calm. I can't imagine what it would be like to leave Styles like this." She stopped and swallowed again when she thought about how soon it could happen.

Maureen put her arm around Rae. "After my divorce, with Trent off at college, this boutique was my life as well as my livelihood. I built it from the ground up. My self-esteem fed off its success. For some years, it defined me. But for a while now, it's been just one dimension of my life. When I walk away today, that dimension will be gone. But I'll still be a whole person."

Back at Styles for her next appointment, Rae thought about what her friend had said. As happy as she was for Maureen, she was feeling sorry for herself. In a purely selfish way, she knew she would miss Maureen desperately.

And she couldn't help wondering how much of a person she would be if she had to give up her business and move out. Because living here in the house and owning Styles was her whole life.

Trent walked back into the empty front room where his mother's boutique had been. Before he could start cleaning up, Rae appeared in the connecting door to Styles.

"Hi," she said.

He smiled a greeting at her, feeling a wave of warmth steal over him, as he always did in her presence.

She stood there in the doorway, hesitating, which made him begin to wonder what she was up to. Stifling a smile, he said, "You wanted something?"

"I...no!" she spluttered. "Well, I mean, yes. I just haven't seen you all day to say hello to. But I also wondered if you had any free time this afternoon."

"You want to go out this afternoon? Come on, Rae, I know very well how busy you're going to be today. You know I check your schedule every morning."

Her face took on a rosy glow. "It's not for me. There are some other people I want you to see."

Trent shook his head. "No."

"No?" Rae was clearly surprised at his lack of cooperation. "Why not?"

"Our deal was that you and I would go out. I never agreed to let myself be exposed to the charms of all the single women in Emerson. So if you are thinking about parading more of them around in front of me, the answer is no."

"Parading! I wasn't..." Rae began indignantly. Then she turned away. "All right. Forget I even asked."

Trent went back to his cleaning, wondering why he felt as if he had pulled a chair out from under Rae when she was about to sit down. After all, he was in the right. And he was tired of being considered Emerson's most eligible bachelor.

The sound of voices in the entryway broke into his thoughts. A little noise wasn't unusual when Styles was busy, but this was different. These were male voices, and they sounded excited, the way pregame locker-room talk did. Trent knew that Rae cut men's hair, too, but they didn't usually arrive all hyped up, or in a pack, or on a beautiful Saturday afternoon.

But they weren't going to Styles. They opened the door to the boutique and tromped in, eleven of them. They literally surrounded Trent.

"Hey, guys. Nice of you to drop by like this." Trent knew very well that something was up, and that Rachel Browning was behind it. The eleven guys standing around him just happened to be Little Ed and Mason and nine other recent grooms who had gone out with Rae. Along with Jim, who was still on his honeymoon, they were the men who had helped Rae earn the nickname of the Groom Maker.

"Come along with us," Little Ed said with grim determination.

"Sure," Trent said with a grin. He didn't really have much choice. He was swept out in the middle of the pack, which came to a halt out on the lawn. "Was there something you wanted?"

Little Ed cleared his throat. Apparently, he had been elected spokesgroom for the bunch. "We just wanted to talk with you is all," he said.

Trent crossed his arms and leaned back against a tree. "Go ahead. Talk."

The locker-room bravado had faded noticeably. Little Ed's face reddened to match the freckles that dotted it. "Well, Trent, the thing is this." Then he gave up and stopped.

Trent laughed out loud. "What did Rae put you guys up to?" he asked.

Little Ed looked relieved. "Hear that, guys? We didn't tell him. He guessed it." He looked at Trent and shrugged. "She wanted us to sell you on the rewards of being a husband."

Trent laughed even harder. "Is that how she put it? 'Sell' me?"

Little Ed scoffed at that. "Nah, of course not. Rae doesn't talk like that. She just thought if we all told you how happy we were married, it might get you to thinking."

"And of course you said you would."

"Of course. Given that Rae is the reason we all ended up so happy."

"Did any of you ever think that you may have gotten married even if you hadn't gone out with Rae?"

All eleven dismissed that with an impromptu chorus of no. Then they fell silent. Trent thought that for a delegation sent to talk with him, they weren't doing much talking. Not that he could blame them. Most guys would go to unbelievable lengths to avoid having to talk about stuff like that. He himself would go double. Personally, he thought Little Ed deserved some kind of prize for even bringing it up.

Trent decided he would put them all out of their misery. While they stood around agonizing, he disappeared into the shed and came out with a softball and a bat. "Hey, how about a game?" he said.

The men took off for the field at the high school. By the time they got there, they had chosen up sides. Two hours later, while they all sat on the ground in left field in the late-afternoon sun, the losing team challenged the winners to a rematch the next week.

Then—and Trent figured Rae had something to do with this, too—their wives started arriving, alone or in pairs, driving or pushing baby strollers, to take them home. In the end, Trent found that he was all alone in left field. The significance of which did not escape him.

Trent walked back home, put the bat and ball back in the shed and got a drink from the hose at the side of the house. He stood there for a minute, wondering at how good it had felt to walk home knowing that Rae would be at the house.

He went inside and poked his head in the door of the salon. "I'm back," he said.

Rae looked over at him with a smile that caused something inside him to cave in.

"Why, hello, Trent," she said. "How was your afternoon?"

There was a customer in the chair and one waiting. "Fine, thanks," he said, happy to have to retreat behind common courtesy. His afternoon had been awesome, thanks in part to her. He disappeared into the adjoining room. Now he could give the boutique that thorough cleaning, as he'd planned, whether or not he could forget the fact that Rae was working just a few yards away from him. In the next room, he was relatively safe from the longing that swelled in him at the sight of her.

He was taking some trash outside later, when the phone rang. Rae came from the other room to answer it. "Styles and—" She stopped, remembering that the boutique was gone now. "Good afternoon, Styles. May I help you?"

"Hello," said a woman's voice. An unfamiliar voice, but a friendly one. "I am trying to reach Trent Colton."

"He's right here. Just a moment." Rae handed the phone to Trent, who had just walked back in.

"Hi, Lee Ann," she heard him say as she went back into Styles.

Trent leaned against the wall in the now-empty boutique. Lee Ann was the woman who wanted to buy the house. True to form, she got right down to business. It was one of the things he liked about her.

"A week from Tuesday looks good for me," she said.

"Great. Then I'll see you here at the house. Noon?"

"Two o'clock is the soonest I can get out there. I have another meeting in the morning."

"Two it is." Trent hung up the phone and started out into the hallway. But something made him stop.

"Where's my change?"

The voice coming from Styles sounded a little too loud and a little too annoyed. He glanced into the salon and saw that it was empty, except for Rae, who stood at the register, and a teenage girl who stood in front of it.

Rae's voice was quiet, but firm. "Your cut was ten dollars, Sara, and you gave me a ten."

"No, I didn't," the girl insisted. "I gave you a twenty. I know, because my father gave it to me this morning. I usually get my hair cut somewhere else, but

I thought I'd come here because it's cheaper and I'd have the other ten to use tonight when I go out."

"Your father may have given you a twenty this morning, but you gave me a ten just now," Rae said, still in a calm voice.

"I can't believe this. You're trying to cheat me."

"Why would I do that, Sara? What would be the point?"

"Ten dollars."

"Pretty lousy reason to lie and cheat someone. I need every dollar I earn, but I don't need a red cent I didn't come by honestly," Rae said.

The girl was silent. Trent listened from the other room, fascinated.

Rae opened the cash drawer again. "I'll tell you what, Sara," she said. "If you are sure you gave me a twenty, why don't you reach right in here and take ten dollars?"

The girl shuffled her feet and mumbled, "Why don't you just give it to me?"

"Because I earned the ten you gave me. If you want ten from me, you'll have to take it yourself."

Sara looked at the ceiling, then at her feet. But she didn't go behind the register. "I just remembered," she said. "I did break the twenty to buy mascara at the apothecary. So I must have given you a ten. I forgot."

Rae gave her a smile of encouragement. "It's all right, Sara. We all forget things. I hope you'll come back to Styles next time you need a haircut."

"You mean you..." The girl seemed somewhat flustered, then she recovered. "Yeah, well, I do like the cut. I can't wait to show my friends."

"It was a pleasure doing business with you."

By now the girl was smiling back at Rae. "Yeah, you, too. Thanks."

When the front door slammed behind the girl, Trent walked into Styles. Rae was still standing behind the register.

"That was really something," he said.

"Thank you."

"You really stood your ground. How did you know it would work?"

Rae opened up the cash drawer so that Trent could look in. There were no twenties.

"You could have proved her wrong at any time."

"If I had, how would she have felt about herself when she walked out that door?"

Trent needed some kind of outlet for his feelings for Rae. He pulled her into his arms. It was such a sweet embrace. She was so sweet.

"What is this for?" Rae asked, although she didn't seem to mind being in his arms.

Trent murmured into her hair, "Anyone else would have been more worried about the money, or indignant at having been called a liar. But you? You gave her a way to save face."

"I'm no saint, Trent. I still got my money."

He laughed. "Yeah. But you're still the closest thing to a saint I know." And that was the trouble. It didn't matter how much he was growing to like her, because she deserved someone who was a heck of a lot closer to sainthood than he was. For some reason, the thought made him want to change the subject. "I can't believe she was capable of trying to steal from you."

Now Rae laughed. "Even I am not *that* naive, Trent. Or is this another affliction you suffer because of your lack of imagination?"

"What do you mean?"

Rae was silent a moment. "I've always believed that each of us is capable of anything."

"Intriguing thought," Trent said. "What are you capable of?"

She gave a short laugh. "Me? I was capable of pulling that exact same scam Sara tried when I was her age, for starters."

If she was trying to shock him, it wasn't going to work. All right, it worked a little. But he made a quick recovery and teased, "I knew I'd find something sordid in your past if I just kept looking. But what about now?"

"If I were as sweet and wonderful as everyone thinks, I would have gotten out of the house just as you wanted me to. I wouldn't have taken the bet," she said. "But as I've told you before, I want this house."

And he wanted her. It was stronger than ever now. He deliberately pulled her closer so that she could feel it, too. "And what do you think I am capable of?" he asked grittily.

She tilted her head back and looked right into his eyes with her rich, coffee brown ones. He didn't know how far she could see into his, but he could see all the way to the center of her warm heart.

"I know that you are capable of being a faithful and loving husband," she said with conviction.

Her words echoed inside him, soul deep, and melted something that had been frozen in there for a long time. He was trying to find the voice to reply, when he heard her next appointment coming in the front door. Which saved him from having to say anything at all.

Chapter Six

Over the next few days, Rae wondered where her conviction that Trent was capable of being a faithful and loving husband had come from. With all the evidence to the contrary, she only had one way of knowing it.

She knew it by heart.

On Tuesday morning, he told her over coffee that he was going to be in Boston for the day to take care of some business. And he asked her out for that evening.

Up until now, she had always been the one to initiate their "dates," at first to make sure he was around other women. Lately to make sure they stayed around Emerson. And he seemed to enjoy doing that.

But this was nice, too—to be asked out, to let him do the planning. It made her feel that he wanted to be with her, regardless of the bet. She wondered what they would be doing tonight.

Trent had said he expected to be back by late afternoon, but when Rae closed Styles at six, he still wasn't home. She took a quick shower, and there was still no sign of him.

Feeling restless, Rae walked out onto the porch. There on the swing she found a box from the florist downtown. It must have been delivered while she was in the shower.

In it were three long-stemmed roses. The note said: "I got held up in Boston, so I won't be picking you up. But our date is still on. Put on your dressiest dress. Your chariot arrives at six-thirty."

Ten minutes from now. Rae swept up the roses and plunked them in the vase in the front hallway. Then she ran up to her room, got changed and had just finished putting her hair up, when she heard a horn sound in the driveway. A spritz of cologne later, she locked up the house and found Little Ed standing in the driveway in front of his grungy old pickup truck, scowling under the hood.

She stopped in her tracks. "This is my chariot?"

Little Ed turned around to answer her, but his jaw dropped before he uttered a sound. He stood staring at her for a full ten seconds.

"What's the matter?" Rae asked, doing a quick check of her dress to see that nothing was wrong with it. She hadn't worn it in a while, but it was basic black, and she had heels on with it.

Little Ed swept off the greasy baseball cap he had been wearing over his unruly red hair. He cleared his throat, but his voice still sounded a mite gritty. "If I wasn't a happily married man, I'd steal you right away from that son of a gun."

Rae blushed, then recovered. "If you'll recall, Little Ed, you had your chance with me already."

"Shoot, you never wore that when we went out."

"You never asked me to wear my dressiest dress when we went out," Rae said with a smile. "So what's the joke? Trent asks me to wear it, then expects me to ride in this old rattletrap with you?"

Little Ed swore under his breath. "I can't blame that on him. He wanted me to pick you up in the limo, the one that Big Ed and I bought after you moved here, when the wedding business picked up so much in this town. But the dang thing had a flat, and I didn't have time to change it, and Caroline was out with the baby in the minivan. This should get us there—if we don't have to sit around in traffic, anyway."

Flowers, the limo...Rae was touched. And curious. "Get us where?"

He dropped the hood and helped her into the passenger seat. "Never mind. I promised Trent I wouldn't tell you. Now, let's get going before we're late."

Rae wasn't surprised when Little Ed drove off in the general direction of Boston. She figured Trent wanted them to meet him somewhere along the way. And if he wanted it to be a surprise, she wasn't going to try to get Little Ed to tell. He was as stubborn as a big red mule, anyway. And she was more curious about the man than the destination.

"Does Trent always go to such lengths for a date?" she asked.

"As far as I know, this is a first," Little Ed said, keeping his eye on the Friday-afternoon traffic.

Rae took that as a good sign.

"You making any progress with him?" Little Ed asked.

"I beg your pardon?" Rae gulped. Was her attraction to Trent that obvious?

Little Ed regarded her curiously. "The bet. How is it going?"

Rae gave a short laugh. "It looks like Trent is winning, so far."

"I take it you haven't gotten him to soften his views on marriage yet."

"Hardly."

Little Ed reached over and patted her hand. "Don't get discouraged, Rae. There's still time."

"Yes," Rae said, forcing a smile. "Still more than two months till the bet is over." She looked out the window and realized they were in Boston. "Boy, Trent doesn't ask for much, does he, having you bring me all the way here during Friday-evening rush hour."

Little Ed laughed. "Don't tell Trent, but this is nothing. I'd hate to have to admit to you the kind of tight places that guy has gotten my behind out of in the past. I'd also hate to remind him, or I'd be spending the better part of the next few years paying up."

He pulled over next to a sidewalk and came to a stop. Rae picked Trent out of the crowd with uncanny accuracy. He had been lounging against a building, hands in pockets, looking deadly handsome in a suit and tie. When they pulled up, he opened Rae's door and helped her down from the cab of the truck. Then he, too, stood looking at her for an excruciatingly long time. "Wow," he said finally.

"That's what I was trying to say when I first saw her," Little Ed said.

"It's just your basic black dress," Rae protested, feeling the color rise in her cheeks.

"Yeah." Little Ed winked knowingly at Trent. "And Ted Williams was just your basic baseball player."

Trent reached into the cab to shake his friend's hand. "Thanks for making the trip, buddy. I owe you one."

Little Ed winked at Rae. "One?" he said to Trent, without a hint of a smile. "I'll put it on your tab." With a growl of the engine, the beat-up truck swung back into the traffic pattern heading out of the city.

Trent took Rae's arm and spoke softly. "Sorry for that lapse into adolescence. If my few wits hadn't scattered when I set eyes on you, I would have given you my best smile and told you that you look breathtaking."

"I got the general message." Rae felt a new blush wash through her cheeks, and glanced away at the people, the cars. She liked the city, even though living there wasn't for her, and she was anticipating spending an evening there with Trent. "Where are we going?"

"How about a concert?" Trent said, holding out a pair of tickets to Rae.

Rae looked at them and then at Trent, feeling her smile stretch her cheeks. "How did you know this would be perfect?"

He shrugged. "I knew you liked music and I knew a guy who had tickets," he said with a grin. "He also had tickets to the game, but I'd hate to think what a dress like that could start in the stands during the seventh-inning stretch."

"I love baseball," Rae said staunchly. "We'll do that another time."

Trent rested his hand against the small of her back as they walked down the block. "I just love a woman who loves baseball," he whispered in her ear.

It would have been easy to be charmed, but Rae caught herself. "I'll put that on my list of qualifications for potential wives for you," she said. "Or maybe I'll hang an Available sign over your seat while we're at the ballpark. Think of the potential for that, especially if you consider the television audience."

"It'd be lots of fun having tryouts, anyway," he said.

Before Rae could think of a comeback, they arrived at the concert, and she surrendered to the night's magic.

And to Trent's.

Afterwards, they walked lazily away in the night air, swinging their linked hands. When they got to his car, Rae settled in and closed her eyes, conjuring up every detail of the night in her head. The setting had been splendid, the music magnificent. But the one thing she was sure she would never forget was the feel of Trent's arm around her.

He was driving slowly, no doubt savoring the night as she was. He had put the top down, and the breeze coming in was a gentle one that accompanied her thoughts perfectly.

Then Rae noticed that it had stopped. So had the car's engine. She opened her eyes and lifted her head up to look at Trent. He was staring out the windshield at a building up ahead.

"What's that?" Rae asked. She sensed that they were still in the city.

"That's my hotel." Trent watched her face carefully, wincing inwardly at the flicker of pain he saw briefly cross her features. He hadn't brought her here to upset her. He was just so excited about the hotel, he wanted to share his happiness with her. It just seemed right to share his dreams—and just about everything else in his life—with Rae.

Rae felt her mouth go dry. "You . . . you've already bought it?"

"My proposal is in, and the owner likes it. It will take a couple of weeks to hammer out the final agreement, and then of course we'll pass papers after my house sale goes through. But it feels like it's mine."

Rae took a good look at it. "I can see why. It's just right," she said honestly. "Not too old, not too new. Not too big, not too small. Not too close to the downtown, not too far out."

Trent smiled. "Not too expensive, either, and that's the key. Everything this building has going for it, five or six others available in the city right now do, too. But this one I can afford, after I sell the Emerson house. This one is the one that will give me my dream, right now."

Rae leaned over and gave him a quick hug. He was so happy about this, it was hard not to feel happy for him. Even when the realization of his dream would mean the end of hers.

Why was life so complicated? Rae wondered as they drove back to Emerson. When Trent pulled up the driveway back at the house, the house she loved and didn't want to leave, she sighed out loud.

"What's wrong?" Trent asked, a frown of concern creasing his forehead.

"Nothing," Rae said, dredging up a smile. As she got out of the car, she reminded herself that the bet wasn't over yet.

Trent stopped her next to the car and stood back to look at her again. The dress she had worn to Jim's wedding had been flowing and romantic, but this one was downright sexy. He had been fighting the effects of it most of the night. "You look absolutely ravishing," he murmured in a low voice, lifting her up to sit on the hood of the car.

Rae felt her eyes lock with his. Neither said anything for a few minutes.

Trent was struggling to keep each new surge of desire at bay. She had such a powerful effect on him. He had been to countless concerts, but tonight was like the first time. She had a way of doing that to him. She was different from any other woman he had ever known, and he wanted to know her better. "Tell me something," he said.

"What do you want to know?" she asked softly.

The night was velvety dark. A cat prowled at the edge of the garden, and a cool breeze began to whisper around Rae's ankles. She crossed them, looking at Trent's profile in the dim light. An intimate note crept into his voice as he asked, "What happened with the other twelve?"

It wasn't a question she had been expecting. Rae thought of all those relationships of the past three years, and of the things she wouldn't tell Trent. Of how she wondered whether she could ever be more than just friends with a man. Of how she had almost given up hope that she would ever do her hair for her own wedding. "What happened? We dated," she said simply.

Trent placed a hand on the hood of the car, next to her hip, leaning toward her. "And?"

Rae shrugged, trying not to show how much his being so close affected her. "And we had a good time. You know them, Trent. They're all nice guys. We had fun."

"So much fun that you stopped seeing them?"

"After a time, it would be obvious that it just wasn't working out," Rae said. "We enjoyed each other's company, but..."

"But what?"

Rae was silent, lost in reflection. The smallest of sighs escaped from her lips, and Trent felt it call up an instinctive response in him. He leaned closer, resting his hands on the car on both sides of her. "Rae," he said, drawing out the one syllable of her name.

"What?"

"Tell me the rest."

Rae took a deep breath. The rest wasn't easy to tell, because it was something she didn't fully understand herself. It was a gut feeling. And though she might not be able to explain it, she knew it was right. "It wasn't a matter of what we had together, but what we didn't have."

"What do you mean?"

"Sometimes, with a few of them, I said to myself, 'Rae, it just doesn't get any better than this. This guy is nice and fun loving and caring and he's looking for someone to share a home and children with, just like you are. What more can you ask for?' And I knew if I just gave him a little encouragement..." She frowned. "I suppose that sounds vain, but—"

"Not vain. Honest."

"Anyway, I could never go further, because there was always something missing."

Something missing. Trent knew what his friends thought was missing, but he also knew that Rae wasn't talking about the physical aspect of those relationships. A woman like her wasn't looking for someone who could give her a good tumble in the hay. She was looking for someone who could take her to the stars.

"Are you talking about *love*, Rae?" he asked. "Is that what was missing for you?"

"As a matter of fact, yes," Rae said with a challenging look.

"Oh, come on! Now, if I were looking to get married—"

"Which, as we know, you are *not*," Rae reminded him.

"True, but if I were, I wouldn't let twelve good prospects go because Cupid didn't shoot me with his arrow, or the stars weren't dancing, or whatever sign of love you seem to be looking for.''

"I don't believe this! *You* are giving *me* advice on how to get married?" Rae said with a laugh.

"Hey, you're the one who *wants* to be married, and had more than one chance to be, and you're not."

"I'm glad I'm not! They weren't the right men for me, any more than I was the right woman for them," she stressed. She had never thought about it in quite that way. At least not consciously. But deep down, she had known none of them was the man for her. Because none of them had broken her heart.

But this man standing in front of her—maybe. Trent just might have the power to break her heart. Oddly enough, at that sudden realization, Rae felt her heart take wing.

As if he had read her thoughts, Trent said, "Come back to earth, Rae."

"Excuse me?"

"Time for a reality check. Did you ever think that maybe you are being overly romantic? It's hard to understand how you could still have stars in your eyes when those eyes have seen romance fail twelve times in the past three years."

To his surprise, a slow smile spread across her face. "You're wrong, Trent. Romance hasn't failed—it's triumphed. Each of those twelve men married the right woman for him."

"But what about you? There are no knights on white chargers, Rae," Trent said, a note of frustration creeping into his voice. "Aren't you worried that you may not ever find this Mr. Right of yours? That he may not even exist?''

Rae resisted the urge to laugh out loud. He existed, all right. As for finding him, that shouldn't be too hard. She'd start by looking right under her nose.

"Oh, yes, I'm worried," she answered in a serious voice. At his look of relief, the corners of her mouth turned up in a mischievous smile. "As worried as I am that the earth will stop turning, the sun will stop shining and the stars will fall from the sky.''

Trent gave up trying to make Rae see reason. He looked up at the sky. "Speaking of stars, they're too beautiful tonight not to enjoy. What do you say we get changed and meet in the backyard?''

Rae slid off the hood of his car and into his arms. "I'm always game for a little stargazing.''

Trent put his arm around her and walked her toward the house. "Who knows," he said hopefully. "Maybe you'll see some fall from the sky.''

"And maybe you'll see some dancing.''

When Rae walked back outside, she saw Trent sitting stretched out on a blanket in the backyard, leaning back on his elbows. She felt suddenly shy, although it was absurd to be so. "May I join you?''

In answer, he patted the blanket and gave her a smile.

Rae settled in next to him, looking at the night sky. "I'm glad you wanted to come out here," she said after a while.

"I haven't seen much of the stars for a while, living in cities.''

"You sound like you've missed them."

"Maybe."

"I'll bet you've missed a lot of other things, without even realizing it."

"Like what?"

"Little Ed, Jim and Mason," she said unhesitatingly.

He grinned. "No one in the world like those lowlifes," he said with affection.

"And your mother."

"Absolutely. She's the best. This is the most time we've spent together since I went to college." He was aware that they were coming to terms with their relationship as two adults. He liked the way it felt.

"And the house?" Rae ventured, wondering if he had sorted out his mixed feelings about it, hoping that he had.

But he didn't answer. He was staring out into the garden, silver edged from the ghostly cast of the sliver of moon that swam among the stars. Then he looked back at her, and the intensity in his gaze made it hard for her to breathe, let alone continue talking.

He reached up and touched her hair. "Take it down?" he asked huskily.

She undid the pins that held it in place and it fell loose to her shoulders. He stroked his fingers through it, sending little tingles through her. After a moment he shifted his hand underneath her hair to stroke the fine, sensitive skin at her nape.

His fingers made her feel things. Unfamiliar things she couldn't put a name to. She made a small sound, three parts sigh and one part moan.

Rae had never felt a strong physical response to any of the other men she had dated. Nothing even approaching what Trent was making her feel now. It was true. None of the others had been the *right* man. And she responded to Trent in a way that went beyond the physical. There was something about him that called to her, and had ever since she had met him. It intrigued her, and made her want to explore it further.

And because she responded to him as to no other man, she hoped he might be the one who could see her for what she was. Not the Groom Maker, but a woman. A woman with her own unique combination of charms and flaws, desires and needs. That in itself was enough to draw her closer to him.

She reached out and ran her hand along his clean-shaven jaw, and was rewarded to see his response to her light touch played out across his face in the semi-darkness. When she traced his cheekbone with her fingertips, he rested his hand on the side of her waist. When her fingertips ran along the edge of his hairline, his hand tightened. And when her fingers grazed his lips, he lost all semblance of control and pulled her into his arms.

It was a shattering kiss for her. She'd never before experienced such stunning need, or felt it in a man. Their lips melded, unreserved, and all the wondering and wanting they had buried during the past weeks suddenly bloomed into a kiss of radiant promise. His warm mouth, his hands sliding up and down her back, taught her more of the power of feelings between a man and a woman than she had ever known existed.

For him, it was a moment of intense relief. He had
been wanting this, and holding back, for so long. Finally, he knew she had felt it, and wanted it, too, and
had given the moment her blessing. He had never
kissed a woman with such feeling and, yes, such rev-
erence. She did that to him.

She did other things to him, too, though; things that
were not reverent at all. He wanted her, with a hunger
more profound than he had ever experienced for a
woman. And this deep, wet kiss that went on and on
was fueling that fire, not quenching it. Rolling her
onto her back, he pulled his lips from hers, reluc-
tantly ending the kiss, and feeling a reluctance in her
that matched his own.

"Rae," he said in a gruff undertone. "You know
where this is heading, don't you?"

Rae looked up at him, her eyes wide. All at once,
she knew. She knew where it was heading, because she
was already there.

She loved him.

Each beat of her pounding heart underscored her
miraculous discovery. Each uneven breath she strug-
gled to take. Each mesmerizing moment her eyes
melted into his.

He watched her breathing unsteadily through parted
lips. Her desire was clearly evident to him, a man of
experience, but the knowledge that she didn't fall into
bed with every man she dated weighed heavily with
him. He wanted nothing better than to be the man who
would awaken her to the joy of lovemaking, but only
if that was what she wanted.

"Don't you?" he repeated. This was no time to hide his intentions. He rolled over on top of her, bracing himself on his elbows so he could look into her eyes, but letting the rest of his body speak for itself. And he made himself wait for her response.

The flood of joy that had overtaken her at the discovery of her love for him began to ebb, slowly, painfully. She didn't need to be a woman of vast experience to know what he wanted. His desire for her was plain. And she didn't need to be a woman of extraordinary insight to know that desire was the only thing he was feeling for her. After all, he had made his feelings about marriage—and love—very clear.

She had finally fallen in love with a man, and she couldn't have made a more unfortunate choice. He might want her body, but he didn't want her love. Getting him to love her back and want to share his life with her—it was hopeless. A hollowness began to spread inside her, filling her, crowding out all other feeling.

She swallowed. "Yes, I know where this is heading. But it's not the way I want to go."

Trent ran the back of his fingers along her cheek, and a shiver ran through Rae. His voice was low and expectant.

"Are you sure? Because those aren't the signals I'm getting from you. I think you want me as much as I want you."

Rae choked back a cry of frustration. He didn't get it at all. It was her honest passion, fueled by her feelings for him, that made her respond to him. It wasn't lust. She loved him, dammit.

"I'm sure," she said, and her voice held both resolve and regret.

Abruptly, he rolled off of her and sat up. She started to get up, but he touched her lightly on the arm to stop her. Sitting, waiting, she looked at him with those fathomless brown eyes. He felt such a powerful pull toward her. And he was tired of playing games.

"I am very, very attracted to you," he said in a low voice. "And I can feel your attraction to me. What's between us is strong. Can't you feel it?"

She didn't answer him, but sat there in the moonlight, looking at the garden as if for solace.

"Rae?"

She swallowed. "Trent, I—" Her voice seemed to crack.

"Please, look at me, Rae."

Slowly, she turned her head, and the eyes that met his were underscored by a glimmering tear poised at the edge of each row of underlashes. They didn't fall, and neither did she wipe them away. "I can feel it, but..."

"But what?"

"It just isn't enough."

Trent felt anger boil up in him. He rolled off the blanket and got up, walking a few steps, swearing under his breath. "What is enough for you, Rae?" he asked, abruptly turning back to face her. "Have you bought into that Groom Maker image? Are you going to spend your life sending men off to other women?"

"You know that is not something I ever wanted," Rae said quietly.

Trent felt stung by regret that he had taken such a cheap shot. He had known from the beginning that Rae was a woman who deserved much more than he was willing to give. But something, maybe guilt, maybe regret, goaded him on.

"Are you going to deny your own honest passion until it withers away?"

"This...passion is all new to me," Rae said, standing up and looking right at him. "I have an idea of what made it grow, but I have no idea whether it will flourish on its own or perish if I deny it."

Her voice softened to a whisper. "But I do know this. I am going to deny it now."

She walked away and disappeared into the house without another word. And although Trent slept under the same roof with her, within the sound of her soft breathing, he had never felt more alone in his life.

The week that followed dragged by after that night, when Rae had felt her runaway emotions crunch to a grinding halt. She believed so strongly in the basics of love, trust, acceptance and belonging—after all, that was why she was the Groom Maker—that she was totally mystified as to why it had been so hard for her to walk away from what Trent was offering. She had always known she wanted a home and family and the secure, nurturing love that went along with it. But she was completely unprepared for the strength of the brand-new longing that Trent had awakened in her, for the passion between a man and a woman.

Of course, Trent hadn't alluded to a commitment of any kind, much less mentioned the word *love*. If a physical relationship was all he wanted, then Rae had done the right thing. She needed to have and give so much more. And he was as far from being anyone's groom as she could imagine.

Neither made further mention of it. It was as if that whole night had dropped out of their past, and they took up as before, dating twice that week, joking about the bet, amicably sharing the house.

Rae showed no visible wounds, but inside, the bleeding still hadn't stopped. All week she had wondered what Trent was thinking.

Trent had never spent a more miserable week in his life. After the night they had come so close, somehow, someway, he and Rae had managed to take a step back. Oh, they had their dates as required by the bet, one to a band concert on the town green, chaperoned by his mother and Hal, and the other to Little Ed's house for dinner. They spent, miraculously, seven long days—and nights—together in the same house. But Trent's control was wearing thin. He wondered how long he could keep up the pretense.

Knowing he should stay away from Rae, but unable to do so, Trent asked her if she would go out to dinner with him that night after she closed the salon. Then he went to take care of some business with his lawyer before the buyer came to look at the house.

Maureen and Little Ed's mother, Darlene, were in Styles that afternoon when a woman stepped into the salon from the hallway. She was about Rae's age, tall and blond and pretty, and dressed professionally.

"Hello," she greeted them pleasantly. Then she saw Trent's mother. "Why, Maureen, how are you?"

"Fine, Lee Ann. I'm flattered that you recognized me after three years. It's nice to see you again."

"It's nice to be here. And you must be Rae."

"Yes. How do you do?" Rae wiped her hand off and held it out to the woman. She recognized the voice from the telephone. This was the woman who was going to turn her beloved house into a restaurant, and Rae was prepared to hate her. But that was hard to do, because Lee Ann happened to be very nice.

"Trent told me about your having to move out. I'm really sorry about that," Lee Ann said sincerely.

"What are you going to do with the place?" Darlene asked her, after they had been introduced.

Lee Ann told them about the chain of restaurants she owned.

"Do you plan to do much demolition?" Maureen asked.

"Oh, no. Mostly expansion. I like to preserve the character and feel of each house I convert."

That should have made Rae feel better.

Lee Ann went on. "This house has a lot going for it, but what separated it from the other places I was looking at were the grounds—they are so lovely and have so much potential—and, of course, the market studies on this area. There's going to be a lot of growth around here in the future, and this will put me in on the ground floor."

"Lee Ann!" Trent said from the doorway. He sounded glad to see her. "You're early. What a nice surprise."

She crossed the room and he greeted her with a genuine hug and a kiss on the cheek. "Hello, Trent," she said. "I was just chatting with Rae and your mother and Darlene."

"Please excuse us, ladies. We have some business to take care of," Trent said.

Rae watched as they left the room. Darlene waited—barely—until they were out of earshot, then she started quizzing Maureen.

"When did you meet her before?"

Maureen cleared her throat. "Trent brought her here once before he went to Tokyo. I believe they were seeing each other at the time."

"Well," said Darlene with a raise of her eyebrow. "She certainly wasn't shy about kissing him in front of his own mother. And he kissed her right back, and him dating you, Rae!"

"Trent is free to go out with other women," Rae stressed. "That is specifically part of the bet."

Darlene looked at her. "You mean that maybe he'll date Lee Ann again?"

"She doesn't seem like Trent's type at all," Maureen said, as if convincing herself.

But she was, Rae thought. She was smart; she was attractive; she was involved with her business. And most important, if he had dated her before, that meant that she was comfortable with his lack of commitment.

She was exactly his type.

Much later, when Rae was doing her end of the day cleanup, Lee Ann came back downstairs and into the salon.

"Trent is making a few phone calls," she said. "Do you mind if I visit with you?"

"Not at all. Please sit down."

Lee Ann took a chair, looking as polished as she had when she had first walked in, hours earlier. She crossed her legs gracefully at the ankles. Rae felt somewhat less attractive than the cleaning rag she still held in her hand.

"Trent told me about the bet," Lee Ann began.

"He did?"

"Yes. He had his lawyer write a contingency into the contract we're going to sign in a few weeks. If you win the bet, he gets out of our sale," she said. "Even though he's sure he's going to win, he said he likes to cover his bets."

"Smart man."

Lee Ann gave her a curious look. "He says you have a reputation around here for turning bachelors into grooms. By some unknown, mysterious means. Is that true?"

"It has been known to happen," Rae admitted.

"Do you think it will work on Trent?"

"I sure hope so. I really want to win the bet."

Lee Ann narrowed her eyes thoughtfully. "If you win, you get to stay here in the house and then get an option to buy."

"That's right."

"So what you really want is to own this house."

"That's why I made the bet," Rae said automatically. But lately, she wondered what she really wanted.

"Well, I want to own it, too, and I will if Trent wins." Lee Ann paused. "Did you know that Trent and I were seeing each other in Boston before he went to Tokyo?"

"I had heard mention of that."

"I was just getting my business rolling then, so marriage was the furthest thing from my mind. But a lot can change in three years," she said, smiling. "What I'm saying is, if you really have some groom-making magic, feel free to use it on me."

Rae looked at her. "I beg your pardon?"

"What I mean is, I wouldn't mind marrying Trent myself. In fact I'd love to. We always did hit it off well. And I wouldn't mind losing the house so much if I got Trent," Lee Ann said with a tilt of her pretty head.

Rae said nothing.

Lee Ann added, in a convincing tone, "You know, Rae, it might be easier to get him married off to me than to someone he's never even met. And you just said how much you want the house."

Before Rae could answer, Trent came into the salon. "Looks like we're all set, Lee Ann," he said.

She smiled up at him. "I was wondering. Do you have any dinner plans, Trent?"

"Rae and I were going to get a bite to eat after she closed up shop."

"In that case, would you mind if I joined you?"

Yes, Trent thought. He minded a great deal. He didn't want to be with anyone but Rae. But Lee Ann had asked, and there was no way to refuse her request, short of rudeness. "Not at all," he said.

"Wonderful," Lee Ann said, smiling up at him pleasantly, but not too eagerly.

Dear God, Rae thought, watching her. It just might work.

"Are you ready, Rae?" Trent asked.

Trent couldn't see Lee Ann behind him, shaking her head, signaling Rae to say no. Rae realized that if she didn't go with them, it might be her best chance to win the bet.

And to lose Trent.

She locked up the register and made her decision. And then the phone rang.

Rae walked into the empty front room. "Good afternoon, Styles," she said into the receiver. After a pause, she said, "Of course, Edna. Come right over."

She came back into the salon. "I've got an emergency. You'll have to go without me."

Trent looked at her in disbelief. "An emergency? Rae, you cut *hair!*"

Lee Ann was giving her a grateful smile. She thought Rae was making it all up so that she could be alone with Trent. "Now, leave her alone, Trent. Men just don't understand this kind of thing," she added to Rae.

But Trent stood his ground. "What's the emergency?"

"Edna Carter just found out that there's going to be a surprise fortieth wedding anniversary party for her and Mr. Carter in the church basement tonight."

"That's an emergency?" Trent asked.

"There's more," Rae said. "Edna tried to give herself a home perm this afternoon, and it didn't take. She's in tears. She said if she has to go looking like there was an explosion on her head, she won't go at all."

"There, you hear that? A bona fide hair emergency." Lee Ann took Trent by the arm and steered him toward the door. On the way out she turned and gave Rae a secret wink. "Goodbye, Rae. And good luck," she said.

And Rae knew she wasn't talking about Edna Carter's perm.

Trent didn't say anything. He just looked at Rae over his shoulder, and then he was gone.

Rae put her head down on the counter. She had been telling everyone, herself included, that what she wanted was the house. Which was a lie. Because all of a sudden, she knew with crystal clarity that there was something she wanted more.

Trent.

But unfortunately, it might be too late for that, and if it was, she had only her accursed groom-making talent to blame. Because when Rae turned off her light at bedtime, Trent still wasn't home.

Chapter Seven

Rae had just woken up, when she heard Trent come whistling down the stairs from the third floor the next morning. He tapped on her door. "You still asleep?"

"How could I be, with all that racket?" she said, hoisting herself out of bed.

"Up and at 'em, Rae. Who knows how many hair emergencies there are out there, waiting for you to come to the rescue?"

"Funny," she said, opening the door to glare at him.

He leaned against the doorjamb, grinning. "Did you save Edna Carter from social embarrassment?"

Rae went over to her dresser and ran a brush through her hair. "Yes, and I was happy to do it."

"I missed you at dinner." He wondered whether she

would have come if she hadn't gotten that last-minute phone call.

"Really?"

"Were you worried about me? I wasn't planning on being out so late," he said. He was hoping for jealousy, but maybe that was too much to ask of Rae. "You must wonder what we were doing." He started down the stairs.

Rae was right behind him. "Unless you were getting engaged, I don't believe it's any of my business."

"Engaged to Lee Ann?" He laughed. "Not a chance."

Rae hunted in the fridge for some orange juice, glad that he wouldn't be able to see the relief on her face. She poured two glasses of juice and handed one to him.

Trent drank his in one gulp. "You didn't get your hopes up, did you?"

"Not a chance," she said.

He handed her a bowl of cereal, and they both sat down to eat. After a few minutes, Trent said, "You want to know what we were really doing all that time? Lee Ann was showing me her—"

"Etchings?" Rae asked, one eyebrow raised in a knowing look.

Trent overlooked her sarcasm, although he took it as a good sign. "Her market research on this area," he explained.

Rae was surprised. "I would think you'd be more interested in market research on Boston, where your hotel will be."

"I am," he said quickly. "But this was interesting, too." Really interesting. Irrelevant to his situation, of course, but interesting all the same.

"She mentioned yesterday that this area is in for a lot of growth," Rae said. "Funny, I never thought about that when I opened Styles here. But as a business owner, I won't be sorry if it happens."

Their eyes met, and Rae looked away first. He knew what she was thinking, because he had just thought of it himself. In two months, she wasn't going to be a business owner anymore.

As soon as the grass dried on Friday morning, Rae went out to the shed. Styles opened late and closed late on Fridays, and Rae wanted to spend this morning outdoors, even though it was threatening rain. It had rained all week, and the grass needed to be cut.

Rae walked back and forth across the yard, the wheels of the mower striping the lawn. She enjoyed pushing the old-fashioned reel mower that had belonged to Trent's grandfather. She hadn't done it for a few weeks. Since he had moved in, Trent had insisted on taking over the yard duties that Rae had done in lieu of paying rent. He said that their bet negated everything about Rae's agreement with Maureen. But Rae had sensed that he had another reason for wanting to do it.

Lately he had been busy around the house, sorting things out and packing them up, some to go into storage in case he wanted them later, some to be sold. He had left the house early that morning to find out about getting a space at the town-wide yard sale to be held on the green in a few weeks.

If Rae hadn't already known she was in love with Trent, she would now, because each day with him was such sweet agony. It wasn't bad enough that the rain had kept them in the house the past couple of days, where she had to endure being so near him. Or that he was waiting to greet her with hot coffee and a warm smile in the morning when she came to breakfast.

He had done what no other man had done for Rae. He had not only accepted her friendship, but had also awakened her passions. And one more thing.

Like the twelve before him, he had taken no for an answer; but unlike them, he hadn't left her. Maybe, just maybe, he thought she was worth waiting for.

Her heart soared at the realization, as she ignored the tiny voice of doubt far below that insisted, "It's because of the bet! He wants the house, not you!"

"Hey! That's my job, remember?"

Rae looked up to see Trent in the driveway, taking some more empty boxes out of the trunk of his car. "You've got enough on your hands," she answered.

He held up the boxes. "Literally. Thanks."

By the time Rae finished the lawn, it had started raining. After she washed up, she got herself a glass of iced tea. Despite the rain, it was warm and sticky out. Wondering what Trent was doing, she poured him a glass, too. It was the most natural thing in the world to be drawn to him, to want to share every small pleasure with him.

She walked all through the first floor and the second floor without finding him. Then she started up the stairs to the attic.

He was stretched out on the landing, next to the built-in bookshelves, thumbing through a book. He looked up at Rae, and the smile that spread across his face sent her heart rocketing to new altitudes.

She sat down on the top stair and handed him the drink.

"Perfect timing," he said. "And I don't mean the iced tea. I need you."

Rae's heart thudded. "To do what?"

"To help me think of a reason I shouldn't get rid of these old books."

Rae laughed. "Whatever reason is making you hesitate is probably reason enough."

"My grandmother would have said something like that. Did I ever tell you that you remind me of her?"

Rae swallowed. "I'm flattered."

Trent smiled. "Tell your average, run-of-the-mill woman that she reminds you of a dead old lady relative, and she'd be insulted."

"I never knew your grandmother, of course, but I know enough about how you felt about her to be flattered. For that matter," she added with an impish grin, "if you want to compare me to your grandfather, go right ahead. I know he was just as dear to you."

"How?"

Rae gave him a gentle smile. "Trent, I live here, remember? I've watched you going around trying to pack up your memories." Memories that, unless she missed her guess, he hadn't quite come to terms with yet.

He leaned back against the stair where she sat. Being here with her had brought back a lot of good memories. Rae had been right, he realized. This house *was* special to him. Because of his grandparents, and because it had been a welcome escape from the unhappiness of his parents' marriage.

Rae reached over and squeezed his shoulder. She meant it as a gesture of understanding for him, but for her it was oddly disquieting. Their touches had been casual and restrained since their kiss under the stars, but beneath the surface hummed an urgency that beckoned Rae to explore. She withdrew her hand. "I'm glad your grandparents left the house to you," she said simply.

"At age nineteen, I wasn't ready to be a home owner. I thought my mom's looking after the place in exchange for having her boutique here was the perfect solution. And it was, for many years."

"Until you came back and found you had all this sorting out to do."

Until he came back and found his dream woman, the one woman who could simultaneously arouse feelings of passion and protection in him, happily settled in the house where he had always found acceptance and security. It was a compelling combination, one that had been warring with his deep-rooted determination to resist just such an attractive lure to settle down. Sorting out? She had no idea of the magnitude of issues he was wrestling with. She who had once said with such naive conviction that he could make a faithful and loving husband.

"You're really happy here, aren't you?" he asked, changing the subject. He answered his own question before she could. "But of course you are. It's obvious. You are the quintessential girl next door. Everyone in town knows and loves you and protects you." Little Ed hadn't been the only one who had tried to warn him off. "And you are so talented in your work. I've watched you—and listened to you—working. Haircutting isn't just an outlet for your creativity. People talk to you, and you listen. You don't just make people look good. You make them feel good."

Rae's voice took on a dreamy quality. "Sometimes it feels like I've lived in this town all my life. The part of Worcester I grew up in was like a small town then. My dad was a barber, and I was always in his shop."

"Sounds like fun."

"It was. My parents were wonderful people who had given up on ever having the children they both wanted desperately. I was born when they were both in their midforties, so I was their miracle baby. Our home was never lacking for love."

"You must miss them."

"The way you miss your grandparents."

He did, although he didn't realize how strong his ties to them had been until recently. It made him curious about the kind of bonding that happened naturally in families.

"Did you get into cutting hair because your father was a barber?"

She smiled. "Maybe, although I didn't realize it at the time. I got my license after high school and cut hair to help put myself through college. After graduation, I worked in business for a while, but that was all wrong for me. But when you have a college degree, you're supposed to aspire to more than just cutting hair."

It was the common assumption, and it sucked. "You're doing what you want to do, and you're happy," Trent remarked. "But it was a gutsy move. That's why I hope you can understand what owning my own hotel means to me." He remembered her reaction when he had driven her by the site he was interested in on the way home from the concert. Pure, unselfish excitement for his excitement, with no allusion to the fact that his attaining his dream would mean hers would be crushed.

"Everything you touch, you turn into a success, Trent."

Everything but his attraction to her. He was miserable with the way things were. He had made a big mistake in thinking that her desire for him might make her willing to compromise her other beliefs. *Everything you touch.* Trent found he wanted to touch her all the time, and not just in the purely sexual way that he had wanted to touch women in the past. He wanted to put his arm around her shoulder, his hand on her hand, his thigh against her thigh, his lips on hers. He wanted to touch her friendship, touch her humor, touch her vulnerability, touch her inner strength. It had been about all he could do to leave her untouched.

"It depends how you measure success," he said finally.

Rae smiled at him, a smile that melted his insides. "Things seem to work out best when you measure it with your own yardstick."

"There you go, talking like my grandmother again."

"Are these her books you're not going to sell?"

She was right, of course. He couldn't sell the books his grandparents had read to him as a child, and that he had later read himself, sitting on this very landing. It would be like selling old friends. Stevenson and Kipling and Longfellow and Aesop. "Hers and my grandpa's."

"Now yours and your grandchildren's."

Trent sighed. "Grandchildren. How they would have loved the thought of having great-great-grandchildren. How they would have loved you, Rae. Grandpa would have said, 'Now, there's the kind of woman you can settle down with, just like your grandma.'" Sitting there in that house, on this stairway landing, with a warm June rain beating on the window and this incredible woman by his side, he could almost convince himself that it could happen. Almost.

Rae spoke softly, but her words held a trace of bitterness that jarred Trent. It reminded him of his own.

"I guess your grandpa didn't know you were the immovable object." She got up and started walking down the stairs.

He remembered how she had said she had never asked for her role as the Groom Maker; she simply was the irresistible force. Well, he was what he was, too.

"I've told you from the beginning. I'm not the marrying kind, Rae," he said after her.

She paused and looked back up at him over her shoulder, and the sadness in her brown eyes made his heart sink.

"Rae?" He needed her to understand what he didn't fully understand himself.

"I'm sorry," she said. "I just can't help wondering what your grandmother would have said to that."

The rain had continued through the afternoon and evening, and business was slow. Rae decided to close up shop a half hour early. No one was going to drive up that muddy lane tonight. She locked the front door and snapped off the porch light.

As she was finishing straightening up the salon, she heard a car in the driveway. She didn't even have to look to know it was Trent's.

He came in the house and stood there in the doorway of the salon with his hands against the frame, looking like a dream in a snug black T-shirt. "I see you're closing up. Would it be too much to ask you to give me a haircut?" he asked.

Wondering what she wouldn't do that this man asked her to, Rae kept her response light. "Double for the trouble, mister. Come on over to the sink."

He did, but first he turned off the overhead lights. Light from a lone floor lamp in the waiting area gave the room a soft glow.

Rae took a clean towel from the pile, trying not to let the intimacy of the lighting permeate her mood. "Trying to save on the electric bill?"

"No. I just want to relax."

"Fine for the wash, but when we get to the cut it may cost you an ear. Have a seat and put this on," she said, reaching for one of her plastic capes.

Trent pulled his T-shirt over his head. "Don't need it," he said.

Rae's breath turned sideways and lodged in her throat. Her fingers slackened and the cape dropped, unnoticed, to the floor. He was magnificent, all male, with sculpted layers of rigid muscles all there for her to see. As her pulse gathered speed, the only coherent thought that formed in her mind was the conviction that he would feel even better than he looked.

Turning away, she got the things she needed out of the cabinet over the sink. She could feel his eyes on her. When she turned back, he was still standing there. "Were you aware that you actually have to sit down to have your hair washed?" she asked, struggling to lighten the mood.

He walked over to the chair, never taking his eyes from hers. Then he sat down, his legs spread wide. The masculinity of the position unnerved Rae. She dragged her eyes up from the faded denim jeans that clung to his thigh muscles like wallpaper, up from the soft furring on his chest that glinted golden in the muted light, to his hair.

She loved the look of it, richly colored in shades that ranged through the browns to the golds. To describe it as sandy didn't do it justice. People would pay big bucks to have the kind of highlights Mother Nature had given Trent free.

Trent cleared his throat. "Don't I have to lean back or something?"

"Not yet. I like to give my customers a cut that works with their hair instead of against it. So first I need to get a feel for your hair's thickness and texture, while it's dry." Rae wasn't sure why she stood there, hesitating. She had wanted to touch Trent's hair for a long time.

And as soon as she did, she abandoned all self-consciousness and gave herself up to the sensations that went through her.

She parted her fingers and pushed them through his hair, slowly, gently, their tips just barely touching his scalp. His thick, clean hair gave way, parting for them, soft and springy and healthy. She did it again. And again. She had never realized just how sensitive the balls of her fingers were, until they began to tingle from the sensation.

Her delicate touch made Trent aware not only that he had nerve endings at the end of each and every hair, but also that they were excruciatingly sensitive. He wondered whether this had been such a hot idea after all. A few minutes of Rae's touch had him wishing that he weren't wearing his oldest, most form-fitting jeans. He shifted in the chair, then dropped his hands strategically to his lap. Dear God, what this woman did to him! And she was only making contact above the shoulders.

Straight ahead of him, he could see Rae's face reflected in a mirror. She seemed unaware of his dilemma, maybe because she seemed to be struggling with sensations of her own. With her eyelids dropped closed, her head tilted slightly to one side, she had a look of pure sensual pleasure on her face. Then he heard his name escape her parted lips, sounding as if it were borne on a puff of steam.

He felt her jolt of awareness at the sound of her own voice. She met his eyes in the mirror, then looked quickly away. Although the light was too low to see it, he was sure that a blush had spread over her cheeks. He had the urge to reach up to touch them, to see if indeed they were warm.

The water started running in the sink behind Trent, and Rae's voice sounded a bit husky as she said, "Now's the time to lean back."

He did, feeling exposed and vulnerable in that position. He closed his eyes, hoping it would help him relax. But they flew back open when he felt her breast press up against his shoulder.

Her eyes went wide. "Sorry," she breathed. "But it's the only way I can..." Her voice trailed off.

He grunted and closed his eyes again, but that didn't get him very far. It only heightened the sensations he was feeling. He could feel Rae leaning over him, and not only the breast that had nestled against his shoulder once more.

The water was the perfect temperature, not too hot or too cold, although Trent knew that even the latter wouldn't have helped his predicament. Still, soft shivers stole along his scalp wherever the water rushed. Then Rae's fingers were back, bathed in lather, massaging with gentle pressure that was both soothing and tormenting. The only thing that drew his attention from them was the thrill that claimed him whenever her breast shifted in its contact with his shoulder.

It seemed to him that she lingered over the shampooing, stroking his hair over and over again. He drew immense satisfaction from the knowledge that she liked touching him as much as he did her. And he was sure she was unaware of the effect she had on him. She was seducing him, but it was an unconscious seduction. Which made the ache even sweeter.

Warm water whispered over his head as she rinsed, her fingers intermingling with its flow. "You can sit up now," she said softly as she turned off the water. She rubbed his hair with a soft, clean-smelling towel. Her breasts were tantalizingly at eye level, and suddenly, some hidden inner dam burst in Trent.

He tossed the towel aside and grabbed her arms. His touch was sudden, but gentle, and Rae had the feeling that he was operating under great restraint. Her own was working overtime squelching the urges that were racing like a brushfire through her right now.

"Do you know how hard it's been to keep away from you?" he breathed, his eyes dark with passion. "Do you have any idea what I'm feeling right now?"

She looked at him, wide-eyed. So it was true. She hadn't imagined his response to her. Given her response to him, that fact was extremely reassuring. And immensely unsettling. She didn't know what to say, so she said nothing.

His eyes roamed her from top to bottom and back again. "Let me show you."

Rae felt a whisper of excitement ripple up her back at his words. Now was the time to say no, to step away, to turn and run and never look back.

She didn't.

He pulled her over in front of where he sat on the chair. She was standing between his legs, and his strong, warm hands began to move slowly up and down her arms, starting a slow burn in her veins.

"Tell me what you feel," he said in a dark voice.

His eyes held hers. She cleared her throat and managed to say, "I feel . . . tingles. Shivery."

He took her hands in his and brought them slowly to his lips. He kissed each one, softly, on the center of the palm, and then rested them on his shoulders. "Tell me what you feel."

Rae ran her palms, moist at first from his kiss, over the smooth skin of his shoulders. Again. Still looking right into his eyes, she said, "You feel warm. I feel the warmth in me." It went from her palms through her arms to somewhere deep within.

Gently, he pulled her down onto his lap, resting one arm across her knees. The other hand he smoothed up her back to her nape, where his fingers stroked her sensitive flesh. "Tell me what you feel."

Her eyes dropped closed, and with a small sound of pleasure she rested her head on his shoulder, her lips against his neck. "I...mmm, buzzing," she breathed. "Humming, inside."

He shifted her on his lap so they were face-to-face, and gazed at her lips. Then slowly, his tongue came out to wet his own. Rae watched with a hunger she had never known. Then he leaned closer and wet her lips that same way. A thrill shot through her at the sweet, warm pressure of his tongue. He sat back and looked at her lips again, his own glistening in the low light, and she knew what it meant to be mesmerized. Finally, he put his lips to hers and rubbed them back and forth, letting the pressure and heat slowly build and then easing off again. His voice was itself a caress. "Tell me what you feel."

"I feel like I want you to... to kiss me."

And then his lips were on hers again, and his tongue followed, and she opened her mouth to gather in his heat. He slid his tongue along hers, and as he repeated the slow thrusts she became addicted to the smooth friction, wanting more. Just when she thought she would die if he stopped, he did, putting his lips to her ear.

"Tell me what you feel," he whispered, his words replete with dark passion.

She swallowed, then ran her tongue over her lips. "I feel..." she breathed. "I feel like I'm... unfolding somehow, way down inside."

With a muffled groan, he kissed her again, hard, and at the same time slid his hand under her shirt. He pushed her bra out of the way and cupped her breast in his palm. Rae was still dealing with the wave of warmth that flooded over her, when he began to run his palm over her nipple, ever so lightly. As touches went, it was no more than a whisper, but it acted as a great awakening cry to every womanly instinct in her. She knew she wouldn't be able to tell him how she felt this time. She would have to show him.

But just before she started, he eased his hand away and gave her a final, soft kiss. As he pulled back, she felt a coolness against her skin, stealing inside.

If he asked her what she was feeling now, she would lie. It was hard enough to die inside without having to describe it.

He didn't say anything right away. He just got them slowly to their feet, holding her steady when she swayed and then releasing her. "I want what we've started here tonight to end very differently," he said roughly. "But you've told me that's not what you want."

Rae stood opposite him, her eyes not moving from his.

When she didn't speak, he went on. "I know one thing you want, though you may not admit it. I can feel it when we touch. You want to fly, and there's no shame in that. Let me teach you," he urged. "Fly with me."

How tempting it was. But not tempting enough. "That's not flying," Rae said, frustrated. "That's just sex. The act is only elevated within the context of a committed relationship."

He took a deep breath. "You really believe in marriage, don't you?"

"Yes." She didn't know what she could say to explain it to him. He would have to figure out for himself what she knew intuitively: that you could never truly fly without first having roots.

"Well, there's the whole problem in a nutshell. Because I don't." His voice had a hard edge to it. "So that's it. End of story."

She took a steadying breath. And another. "You can't be the same man who has lived in this house with me, who has shown he cared in so many ways, not only for me, but for the values that make life worth living, and tell me you don't know how this story should really end. I feel something in you, too."

He said nothing, so Rae went on. "As far as your preferring to live alone, or not wanting to be tied down, or any of your other timeworn male-posturing reasons for not wanting to get married, let me tell you, I don't buy any of them. If you don't know the real reason you're afraid to commit to me, then it's about time you thought about it."

She turned to walk away, but his voice stopped her.

"Oh, I know the reason, all right. You want me to say it? All right, I'll say it. It's that it would kill me to do to you what my father did to my mother."

She turned around to face him, speaking slowly and precisely. "You are not your father."

"Save your pop psychology for the people whose hair you get around to cutting," he said softly. "I know I'm not my father. But I also know I've never been with a woman for more than a short time, and you deserve better."

"None of them was the right woman. I am."

He swore fiercely. "I know. All the more reason not to risk hurting you."

What did he think he was doing to her now? she wondered. She willed herself to calm. "Then you must think it's a risk for me, too. But I don't. I have no fear that our marriage would be like that of your parents. Theirs was a mistake, but that doesn't mean all marriages are, Trent. Look at how happy your mother is with Hal. Think of your grandparents. Those are your roots, too.''

He didn't come right back at her with a response. He seemed to be listening to her, so she went on. ''Most things in life come with a risk. But you can't open yourself up to the rewards of life unless you allow yourself to be vulnerable. If marrying you is a risk, it's a risk I'd gladly dare.''

''God, Rae, can't you see how hard this is for me?'' he said in a tortured voice. ''It's because I feel so strongly for you that I can't marry you.''

Her heart was in her eyes as she answered, ''And it's because I love you, too, that I can't let you settle for anything less.''

Chapter Eight

It was no wonder Rae slept through her alarm the next morning.

After her last words to Trent, she had walked away, up the stairs and into her room, where she curled up into a ball under her covers. She finally gave way to the tension of the past few weeks and slept like a dead woman, oblivious to the world beyond the edges of her bed.

As a refuge it had been highly effective, but only temporary. She opened her eyes to full sunlight in the room and saw by the clock that she had five minutes to pull herself together enough to open Styles and work her way through a full Saturday schedule. Five minutes until she might run into Trent in the hallway or the kitchen.

But she didn't. He was at the house until late afternoon, when the guys came to get him for a softball game. But he steered clear of the salon. Rae was glad not to have to face him after what had happened the night before.

Never since opening Styles had Rae spent the day counting the hours until closing. Today she counted the minutes. When she finally closed the door behind the last customer of the day, the phone rang. It was Little Ed. After playing softball, the guys had gone to his house for a cookout, and their wives and families were joining them.

"Trent is out getting some stuff we need, so I thought I'd go ahead and give you a call," said Little Ed in his booming voice. "Why don't you come on over?"

Rae took a deep breath. "Thanks for asking, Little Ed, but I have something to take care of here. Please give everyone my best."

"Are you sure?" Little Ed prodded. "We're all going to miss you. Especially Trent."

No, Rae thought, he of all people would miss her the least. He had made his choice. And he had not chosen her.

After she hung up, Rae walked through each room of the house she loved. She wasn't prepared for the pain that assailed her. Trent might as well have been there after all, his presence was so strong, his absence so marked.

One thing was very clear. She was not going to live in the house a minute longer than she had to.

As she packed, feeling pain wash over her in waves, Rae made some promises to herself. She was closing this chapter in her life immediately. Of course, Styles would fold. She would go to work for someone else, somewhere else. She'd begin saving again, and hope for a new start in a business of her own, at some time in the distant future. If she was very, very lucky.

This house meant a lot to Rae. In fact, a few short weeks ago, when Trent had first come to Emerson, living and working there was unquestionably the most important thing in her life.

But what did the house matter now? Now that she knew she would never have the man she loved.

Trent felt as though he'd spent the entire cookout dodging questions about Rae. He'd stayed to help Little Ed clean up afterward, so it was late when he pulled into the driveway back at his house. It was late, but Rae's car wasn't there. In the kitchen, where they usually left notes for each other, there was one waiting for him. When he unfolded it, a key dropped to the floor with a ringing clatter that seemed to echo in the empty house. The paper held just one line of Rae's handwriting. "The bet's over," it said, "and you've won."

Trent stared at the piece of paper for a few minutes, as if he expected more words to appear. Then he spat out a one-syllable oath, crushed the note in his fist and tossed it angrily into the trash can.

The next morning he was standing in Styles, looking around at the salon that Rae had built, when he heard a knock at the front door.

It was his mother, and judging by the disappointed look on her face, he guessed she had heard from Rae.

"I just got off the phone with Rae," she began, after Trent had poured them each a cup of coffee in the kitchen. She paused, as if expecting him to say something. He didn't.

"I was surprised to hear that she had left town," she said.

"It was a surprise to me, too," he said flatly.

"Odd, that she would leave so suddenly. She always seemed so happy here. Do you have any idea why she would leave?"

"No, and I don't know why you think I should," he said testily.

Maureen gave him a rare taste of her gently delivered sarcasm. "No, I don't know why, either. Given that you have been living in the same house with her and dating her."

"We were dating because of the bet," he reminded her. Which was true, although he guessed that at the end, the bet had been as far from Rae's mind as it had been from his. "You're her best friend," he stated to Maureen. "More likely she'd tell you."

"Well, she didn't."

At least he could be thankful for Rae's integrity on that point, Trent thought moodily. Whatever had happened between them would stay between them and not become fodder for all the gossips in town. If she hadn't talked to Maureen, she certainly wouldn't talk to anyone else. He gave his mother a direct look and said, "Then I guess Rae has her reasons, and they're her own business."

"I suppose, although it's hard to imagine why she would leave now, before she had to."

He had thought of that, too. In leaving, Rae had sacrificed everything that meant the most to her— Emerson, her business, the house. Everything but her utter and absolute belief in love.

"Maybe she didn't want to prolong the inevitable," he said to his mother, not believing his own words.

"I know you think you were going to win the bet, but Rae would be the last person to give up hope. And even if she had eventually lost, I doubt she would have cut all ties to Emerson like this. I couldn't even get her to tell me where she was." Maureen sat back in her chair, looking steadily at Trent. He recognized that look. It looked the same over the rim of a coffee mug as it used to over the edge of his cereal bowl when he was a kid. It was her concerned look.

When he didn't say anything more, she spoke again. "I want you to know that I have no intention of getting in the middle of whatever is going on between you two," she said. "But when I told Rae I was coming over here this morning, she asked me to give you a message."

Trent kept his face impassive, although his heart started beating double time. "Yeah?"

"She said to tell you that Little Ed and Mason would be coming over later to clear the heavy things out of Styles that she couldn't move herself and..." Stopping, Maureen gave him a curious look. "Trent? What is it?"

"Nothing. What else did she say?"

"She asked me to give Little Ed the key she left you if you weren't going to be home. That's all."

Of course that was all, he thought. What else could he expect Rae to say? That he was right and she was wrong? That she had changed her mind about everything she believed in?

"So will you be here, Trent?" his mother asked.

Slowly, imperceptibly, he let out a breath he hadn't been aware he was holding. "I'll be here," he said.

When Little Ed stalked up the walk that afternoon Trent didn't even need to see the look on his face to know that his big friend was loaded for bear.

Sure enough, Little Ed was barely in the door before he lit into him. "What the hell did you do to her?" he asked without preamble.

Trent never flinched. "Nothing, not that it's any of your damn business," he said, crossing his arms.

Little Ed stood nose to nose with him. "I knew you were going to break her heart. I ought to break your face."

"You could try," Trent said in a low voice that vibrated with warning.

Just then, Mason appeared in the doorway. At the same time, Little Ed and Trent took a half step apart.

Mason's brow was furrowed with concern. "Jeez, I hope Rae is all right. Does anyone know where she is?"

"Not me," said Trent.

"Me, either," Little Ed admitted. "But wherever she is, she's probably better off." He glared at Trent.

"I think that's a safe assumption," Trent said evenly. "Given that leaving here was her idea."

"Was it?" Mason asked. "I have to admit I wondered, given that getting her out of the house has been your objective all along."

Now Trent bristled at him. "Are you implying that I forced her out?" he challenged.

"Not at all," Mason answered diplomatically. "But I did think that it was possible that if the bet wasn't working, you two might have come to some other agreement about the house."

Trent brought his flaring temper under control. "Look, she just decided to move out. I don't know why everyone is so concerned about it."

"Maybe it's because we know she was in love with you," Mason said matter-of-factly.

"Why the *hell* would you think that?"

"Maybe because Rae is such a sensitive and caring person that something like that would naturally be written all over her."

"Look, I never led her on. I told her from the beginning, in front of the whole damn town, including both of you, that I am not the kind of man who commits himself to a woman."

"Sounding a mite defensive..." Little Ed put in from the sidelines, through clenched teeth.

"Have you thought about talking to her?" Mason suggested quietly.

"It would be awfully hard to talk to someone who has left without a trace," Trent reminded him in a voice of acid. "Now, can we stop talking and get this stuff in the truck?"

When they finished loading his pickup, a still-hostile Little Ed slammed the tailgate closed. Then he pulled Trent aside for a final word. "Look, you and me, we've been through a lot together. I want you to know that I'm not only pissed off because I think you hurt Rae, I'm also pissed off because I'm standing here watching my best friend throw away the best thing that ever has or will come into his life, and the damn fool doesn't even know it."

Trent set his jaw. "I'll say it one more time. Rae is the one who left."

"And you're sure as hell not going to crawl—is that it?" Little Ed said, shaking his head. The anger in his voice had given way to sadness. "They say I'm stubborn, Colton, but you wrote the book. I guess I can understand why Rae wouldn't be able to live with you."

As he climbed into the truck, he added over his shoulder, "I just hope you can live without her."

He could live without her, all right. It had been hell living *with* her, Trent thought as the truck pulled away. Rae was an attractive woman. It was only natural that just being near her had been enough to awaken a desire in him that had built to a near-explosive level of frustration. Not surprising, he reasoned, since all that lust hadn't had an outlet. It would be easier now that she wasn't right there in front of him, her very presence a sweet temptation. Not only that. With her gone, now there was nothing standing in the way of his plans to sell his house. The bet was over. He could go on with his life.

When he walked back into the house, he deliberately kept his eyes from the empty room where her salon had been. But it didn't stop him from thinking of how it, and the rest of the house, had once been so full of Rae's laughter. And her caring. And her dreams.

Staring those memories of her in the face sure put a slow leak in his balloon of cynicism.

Rae spent Saturday night at a cheap motel. With her phone calls to Maureen and Little Ed on Sunday morning, all of her arrangements to move were finished. Little Ed would store her Styles equipment at the garage until she could make arrangements to sell it. Next she contacted her old boss, Victor, who was sorry that Styles had folded, but pleased to have her come back to work for him. She spent Sunday evening unpacking in the room she had rented over Victor's salon.

It wasn't a great room. In fact, even Rae had to admit that it was a pretty crummy room. But it was close to work, it was cheap and it was available.

On Tuesday, when she walked through the door of the salon to work, Rae plastered a smile on her face. She did it for one reason and one reason only—she owed it to Victor and to his customers to be pleasant. This was her life now, and she was determined to be happy with it, just as she had always done in the past.

But in the past, she hadn't known what it was to love Trent. The truth was that although she kept it hidden from those around her, that first day and the days that followed were misery for Rae.

But even while it grieved for Trent, her heart insisted that she had done the only thing she could do.

On a Monday morning two weeks later, Trent went to Boston, to sign the purchase and sale agreement on the Emerson house with Lee Ann and to finalize his offer on the hotel. He had slept badly the night before—as he had every night since Rae had left—so he had come into the city early. Now, with time to kill before his meetings, he found himself pacing the sidewalk in front of the hotel that was soon to be his, hands in his pockets.

Everything was falling into place for Trent, and soon he would have what he had wanted for so long. While he was working toward it, he had wondered how he would feel now, when he was literally standing at the doorstep of his dream. Would he be proud, euphoric, content?

But he felt none of those things, only the same numbing, chilling emptiness that had been gnawing at his insides for weeks.

At first he had told himself that it was because of Emerson. Coming home, he had become a part of things there again. It had felt good being back at the house, and being with his mom and his buddies. As far as he had gone, his roots *were* there, and he was smart enough to realize that he was going to miss that connectedness when he left once more. He never would have guessed that returning to the simple pleasures of hometown living could so greatly reduce the appeal that cosmopolitan life had always held for him. Even so, that wasn't enough to make him want to change his mind about his future.

He turned to look at the building where his future would unfold. But after a moment or two, his interest flagged and his gaze turned unseeing. A movement down the sidewalk captured his attention. Walking toward him was a woman, one of the first of the morning commuters to be up and about. Her appearance was appealing, her demeanor professional, and she smiled confidently at Trent as she walked past him and entered the building next to his, briefcase in hand. It looked as though they were going to be neighbors, and Trent's male instincts told him that they could become something more.

But instead of anticipation, he felt a jolt of repugnance at the thought. And it wasn't too hard to figure out why. He had admitted to himself a long time ago that Rae was the only woman he wanted, and that fact had only become truer over time. He missed her with a visceral fierceness, as though something had been torn from himself. Nothing was the same without her. She had brought meaning to his life that he hadn't even realized was lacking.

And she loved him. Her telling him that on their last night together had filled him with anger, because he had never meant to hurt her. But it had also filled him with wonder. She *loved* him. And he was still trying to come to grips with it. He resumed pacing, his brow creased in thought. Being loved by a woman like Rae was not something a man could take lightly. Trent couldn't. A commitment to Rae was a commitment that would go even deeper than marriage vows. The man Rae loved would have to give her his body, mind, heart and soul, wholly and unreservedly.

He had convinced himself not to commit to her because he was afraid of hurting her. But by rejecting her love, he had done that anyway. He had let both of them down. The fact that he had been going through hell since she'd left wasn't lost on him. He couldn't imagine what she had gone through.

And suddenly, finding that out mattered a great deal.

"Mr. Colton! You're early."

Trent shook hands with the man he had come to meet with and waited while the man unlocked the building and ushered him inside. The man was smiling now, but Trent knew he wouldn't be for long.

After Trent withdrew his offer on the building, he met with Lee Ann and told her he had decided not to sell the house in Emerson. Lee Ann was not happy, either, but after their meeting she was convinced that nothing was going to change his mind.

And she was right. Trent was going full speed ahead, in a completely different direction. It had been surprisingly easy to scrap his carefully laid plans. Not that owning the hotel hadn't been important to him; it had. Then. But now, only one thing in the world mattered to Trent.

And he didn't even know where she was.

Well, it was damn well time to start looking, he thought as he drove away, leaving Boston far behind.

After the salon closed that Wednesday, Rae gathered all her loose change and went to the pay phone in the corner of the shop to call Little Ed. She hadn't told anyone her whereabouts, because she knew her friends in Emerson too well. They knew she wouldn't take charity, but as out-of-the-way as the salon where she was working was for them, they would still come to her for haircuts. She simply couldn't let them do that. But she missed them, and was desperate to hear a familiar voice.

"Yo." Little Ed answered the phone in a loud voice, to carry over all the background noise in the garage.

"Hi, Little Ed. It's Rae."

"Rae! It's about time you called! Are you all right?"

"I'm fine. Everything is just . . . fine. I just wanted to say, have a happy Fourth of July tomorrow. How is everything in Emerson?"

"Oh, the same, except we're a sorry bunch without you. You better come back soon. Everyone's hair will be looking like hell before long."

Rae laughed, and it felt so good. "Little Ed, your hair always looked like that anyway, so don't go blaming me."

"Aw jeez, Rae, I mean it," he said. "How about coming back? We'll all help you find another place to put Styles. Hell, you can have the back corner of the garage if you want, right behind the grease pit. People can get their oil changed and their hair cut all in one trip."

Rae felt her smile start to crumble. He was so dear. They all were.

"Mason and Jim and all our mothers have been asking about you. And all the other grooms and all the wives and all the single women who think they'll never get married now that you've left Emerson. And Hal and Maureen and . . ."

Little Ed paused, and lowered his voice. "What the hell did that son of a gun do to you anyway, Rae? Just say the word, and I'll clean his clock for you. He could use it—let me tell you. He's been haunting everyone in town the past two days, trying to find out where you are. Shoot, here he is now."

The muffled silence that followed on Little Ed's end was swallowed up by Rae's heart pounding in her ears.

Trent was there at the garage. Then all of a sudden he was right on the other end of the phone line.

"Rae." His voice was low.

"Trent." She clutched the phone tighter. How could his voice, the thought of him, still affect her like this?

The answer was plain enough. She still loved him.

"How are you? *Where* are you?" he said, sounding like he was keeping his voice low only with great effort. "I've been trying to get in touch with you, but no one here will tell me anything."

"No one there knows anything. I wanted it this way."

"Well, I don't. I want to see you again."

"No." She didn't know what she would do if she saw him again. Just hearing him was torture enough. "I need to start over. I think it's for the best."

"We need to talk," he insisted.

"I have nothing else to say."

"Then listen."

Rae swallowed. "I've got to go," she said softly.

"If you won't tell me where you are, will you at least call me back?"

"No." She wouldn't lie to him or leave him hanging. It was better this way. "I wish you all the best. Goodbye, Trent." With shaking hands, she cradled the phone.

When Trent heard the soft click in his ear he slammed down the phone he was holding. He couldn't blame her for not wanting to talk with him. She had every right to be angry, to be hurt, to doubt. And he doubted that anything he could say would make a difference.

* * *

Friday evening was busy at Victor's salon. During a lull Rae went to the deli down the street for a grinder. She was glad it was so busy, she thought, stretching her tired legs out in front of her as she picked at the sandwich. Yesterday had been the longest holiday off she had ever spent. But when she was busy, like tonight, she didn't think about Trent as much.

Ha. Who was she trying to kid? she wondered. She thought about him constantly, and no wonder. When she found Trent, she had felt a completion to her life that she hadn't realized she'd needed. She now understood what people meant when they used the term *soul mate*.

And what did soul mates do? They complemented each other, building on their strengths and helping each other overcome their weaknesses. Trent had made a mistake. He had hurt her badly. But she had let him down, too, by not giving him the chance to make up for the hurt. She could have listened to him on the phone on Wednesday. Should have.

She trudged back into the salon, heartsick and weary. There were still no appointments for her, but she had to be ready for walk-ins. She started sweeping up around her chair.

"I'd like a haircut. With Rae."

Her head jerked up at the sound of that familiar voice. Trent had found her. He was standing next to the front counter, looking right at her, his hazel eyes dark with emotion and underscored by shadows. He looked as if he hadn't slept in days.

"Rae? Oh, you mean Rachel? Right that way, sir," Victor said, pointing him back to where Rae stood with the broom still in her hand, rooted to the floor.

Trent walked over and sat in her chair. "So you're back to 'Rachel' again?"

She met his eyes in the mirror. "This isn't Emerson," she said.

"No, it isn't."

Rae put the broom away and came back to stand next to him. "You . . . you really want a haircut?"

"I've needed one for a while, but we didn't get past the shampoo last time," he said huskily.

He didn't have to remind her of that. The memory of that night was all too clear. Rae put her hands on the back of the chair to stop their shaking.

He still held her eyes with his in the mirror. "I would have been here sooner, but it took me this long to track you down."

"How did you?"

"Let's just say I've been in most of the salons in three counties. Not to mention spending yesterday going crazy because everything was closed for the holiday."

Rae felt emotion choking her. She tried to step away, but he spun around and grabbed her by the arms, turning her gently to face him.

"And if I hadn't found you tonight, I would have kept on looking," he said, letting her look right into his eyes and straight to his soul.

Rae backed away again, and he let her go. "I can't cut your hair," she said softly, her voice shaking.

"I'm very glad to hear that," he said slowly, his voice full of meaning. "But that's not really why I came. I want you to come with me."

"You want to talk?"

"No. There is something I'd like to show you."

"I can't leave. I'm working for another two hours."

Trent got up off the chair and went back to where Victor sat at the front, leading the crowd in openly staring at them. "How many more haircuts would Rae be doing for you during the next two hours?" Trent asked, looking at the price list.

"Depends on how many people walk through the door," Victor said.

"What's the most?"

Victor shrugged. "Tonight? Three."

Trent took out his wallet and slapped a wad of bills onto the counter.

Victor's eyes bulged, then he turned to Rae. "You've got the rest of the night off," he said. "And some of tomorrow morning, too."

"I don't believe this!" Rae said, looking at Trent in astonishment. "You're *paying* him for me?"

"No. I've just arranged a night off for you. What you do with it is your business." He smiled at the crowd, which was hanging on every word. "Good night, all," he said, and walked out the door.

Rae stood with her mouth agape for a count of ten before following him out. A lusty cheer rose up from her co-workers and the customers.

Trent was sitting in his car, which was parked right outside. The top was down, and he was staring off into the distance. She opened the door and slid into the seat beside him.

He looked at her. "Are you sure this is how you want to spend your night off?"

She cleared her throat. "What did you have in mind?"

"I want to take you for a drive."

"That's it? Just a drive?"

He nodded. "As I said, there's something I'd like to show you."

He wasn't pushing—he was just asking. It would be hard to say no. "All right," she said.

He started up the engine and pulled away from the curb. Warm evening air poured around them. Trent wasn't saying anything, and Rae wasn't in the mood to make small talk. She looked out at the scenery rushing past. They came to Worcester and went through it. Rae recognized the road they were on, and couldn't help smiling a small smile. "Are you by any chance kidnapping me and taking me to Emerson?"

"No. But don't think I hadn't thought of that," he said, letting a smile touch his lips for the briefest instant. Then he added soberly, "Rae, you're in charge here. If you change your mind and want to go back, I'll take you. I'll take you wherever you want, whenever you want. Just say the word."

Rae fell silent. A few miles closer to Emerson, Trent pulled over to the side of the road. Sitting a ways back, among a stand of trees, was a large white estate house.

"Is that what you wanted to show me?"

"Yes."

Aware that he was watching her, Rae looked at the building. Even in the twilight, she could see that it was a wonderful old place, if in need of some repair. "It looks familiar," she said.

"My great-grandfather hired the same builder for it that he did for the house in Emerson."

"This house was in the Colton family, too?"

Trent nodded. "In his will, he gave the Emerson one to my grandfather and this one to his elder son. My great-uncle Jacob."

"Is he still alive?"

"Still alive and still owns it. I found that out the time we ran into my cousin Gina, his granddaughter. Since then, I've found out that he's also a shrewd businessman." Trent paused and then said, "He'll make me a good partner."

Rae's voice cracked. "Partner?"

Trent nodded. "We've decided this is the perfect location for our inn. Right on Worcester's doorstep, yet far enough away to be peaceful. Smack-dab in the middle of the projected growth Lee Ann's market research showed."

Rae was shocked. "But what about *your* hotel—the place in Boston?"

"Some dreams are even better when you share them," he said, looking at her meaningfully. "This inn will be a family business. I'll manage it, and Gina will work the desk while I'm training her."

His voice lowered. "Besides, Boston would be too far to commute to from Emerson."

"But I thought you were going to be living in your condo in Boston."

Without a word, he handed her a page torn out of a Boston newspaper's classified listing, dated that morning. There was an entry circled under Condos for Sale, Boston.

Rae read it and looked up at him. "Yours?"

"Mine. The money will be my stake in the inn."

He wasn't going to live in Boston. He was going to live in Emerson. "Then you're not selling the house?"

"I can't sell the house," he said simply.

She grabbed the hand he had resting on the stick shift and gave it a squeeze. "I'm so happy for you, Trent," she said. "And your grandparents would be thrilled. You'll be living in the house. You've come home to your roots. I knew you couldn't sell the house."

"All that is true, but I really meant that I *can't* sell the house."

Rae looked at him, confused. "What do you mean?"

He took her hand, absently brushing the back of it with his fingers. "Well, we agreed that you would have the option to buy it in two years, so I really can't sell it to someone else now."

Rae's eyebrows puckered. "But Trent, that was if I won the bet."

"You will win the bet," he said, bringing her hand to his lips. "If you say yes."

"What?" Rae mouthed the word, but no sound came out.

He captured her mouth in an achingly tender kiss that left no doubt as to his meaning. "I probably should be on my knees in a moonlit garden with flowers and champagne and a diamond ring, but I couldn't wait."

He kissed her again. "I love you," he whispered huskily. "But it took me a while to figure it out, even after the night when you said you loved me, *too*. How did you know?"

It had been obvious. "Because your biggest concern was not hurting me," she said softly.

"I won't," he promised, his voice heavy with emotion. "But I will love and cherish you for the rest of our lives, if you marry me. Will you?"

Rae saw the love in his eyes, felt it in his touch. "Yes," she said, when she could finally speak. "Trent Colton, you're all I want." Then she hugged him, fiercely, and felt something leap up inside her to bind with him. She never, ever wanted to let go. He must not, either, because he didn't for a long time.

Eventually, he pried her head away from his shoulder and she turned her tearful eyes up to meet his. "Do you know what I want?" he said. "I want us to live in that house forever. I want our roots to grow long and strong, together." He stopped for a moment, and his voice dropped to a whisper. "What about you, Rae?"

She didn't have to think. She just let her heart do the talking. "Me? I'm ready to fly."

A few minutes later, the car set off down the road toward Emerson, and home.

Epilogue

The diamond ring that Trent's grandfather had once given his grandmother fit Rae perfectly, and she wore it for two weeks. Then one hot Saturday in July, Rae did her hair for her own wedding, with flowers from the garden, and a new gold band nestled next to the antique diamond. She had made Trent a groom, but more important, he had made her his wife.

Little Ed, looking suitably uncomfortable in a tie, was best man, and Maureen was resplendent in her dual role as mother of the groom and matron of honor.

After the ceremony, the whole town was invited back to Trent's house. Everyone was there—the twelve former grooms and their brides, the mothers, Trent's uncle Jacob and cousin Gina, Rae's customers, Trent's football buddies and the women Rae had tried to fix him up with. The high-school jazz band played background music as the grown-ups drank punch and the kids chased one another among the trees.

When Rae and Trent walked onto the lawn, Maureen came up to Rae and gave her a big, genuine hug. Her voice was full of emotion. "Since I met you, you've been like a daughter to me. Now you are my daughter."

Rae hadn't thought about that before. She not only had Trent, she was part of a family again. "I'm so happy," she whispered.

Maureen passed her to Hal for a hug, and then Trent grabbed his mother for one. As the crowd gathered around them, congratulations and good wishes rained on the bride and groom.

The mothers of his friends were the first ones to move in on them for hugs. "Didn't I tell you?" Little Ed's mother, Darlene, chortled with glee. "I knew from the first time I saw them together at Jim's wedding that this would happen."

"Good for you, Rae!" Mason's mother chimed in. "If anyone could have gotten this boy to change his ridiculous notions about marriage, it was you."

"If you want to know what I think," added Jim's mother, beaming, "I think this ending is right out of a storybook. That's what I think."

When they all started talking about Rae's ring and gown, their sons pulled Trent aside.

"I guess we know what happens when the irresistible force meets the immovable object," Little Ed said with a laugh, slapping Trent on the back.

"How does it taste to eat your words?" Mason asked, grinning.

Jim shook his head. "So this is what comes of a sacred oath sworn on a classic convertible," he said with mock solemnity. Then he brightened. "Oh, well, if you need any ideas for your honeymoon—"

Little Ed broke in with a booming laugh. "Are you kidding? He's been having those ideas since he first set eyes on Rae."

Trent grinned. What his friend said was true. But it was also true that the overwhelming feelings of frustration he'd been battling weren't from not having an outlet for his lust, but from not having one for his love.

And now that he did, it was a relief to let that love burst forth in a tidal wave. He felt lit up from the inside.

How he loved her. She had been right about that, and about something else, too. He *was* going to be a great husband. He really did feel capable of anything.

He went to get his wife. When they stood up on the porch, a cheer went up from the crowd gathered below on the lawn.

"Hey, Rae, you did it!" Little Ed called. "You made a groom out of that son of a gun, and the three months aren't up yet!"

Everyone clapped and whistled, even the ones who couldn't resist the odds and had bet against Rae. There was a lot of laughter as money changed hands.

"You better make sure he pays up, Rae," Little Ed warned her.

"Don't worry. Styles is going to stay right here in the house," Trent said.

"*And* she gets to buy you out in two years," his friend reminded him. "Those were the terms of the bet."

"But Rae doesn't want the house anymore," Trent said innocently. "She just wants me." He smiled at the hoots that went up from the crowd and turned to Rae. "Don't you?" he asked her.

The crowd quieted to hear her answer. Rae smiled softly. "He's right," she admitted to the whole town of Emerson. "All I want is my husband."

All of the women, and more than a few of the men, reached for handkerchiefs. Trent put his arm around Rae and reached into his suit-jacket pocket. But he didn't pull out a handkerchief. "Then I guess I didn't have to go ahead and do this," he said, handing her an envelope.

Rae's eyes widened as she unfolded the piece of paper she found inside. It was the deed to the house. On it were the names Thomas Trent Colton, Jr. and Rachel Browning Colton. They owned the house together now. "No, you didn't have to," she said, in a voice full of emotion. "But I'm honored that you did." Then she kissed him.

The crowd cheered again, then parted. From around the corner of the house came Mason's mom, pushing a cart holding the wedding cake she had made to look like Rae and Trent's house.

Later, while the guests were talking and laughing and eating wedding cake, Trent came and stood behind Rae on the lawn. While they both looked up at the house, he wrapped his arms around her waist and murmured in her ear, "What do you say we fill this old place to the roof with babies and grandchildren?"

Rae's soft smile turned saucy. "Enough talk, Mr. Colton. Are you ready for some action?"

Trent swept her into his arms and started for the porch. "You can bet the house on it, Mrs. Colton," he growled, as he carried her over the threshold.

* * * * *

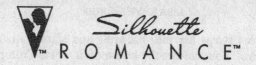

COMING NEXT MONTH

#1108 THE DAD NEXT DOOR—Kasey Michaels
Fabulous Fathers
Quinn Patrick moved in only to find trouble next door—in the
form of lovely neighbor Maddie Pemberton and her son, Dillon.
Was this confirmed bachelor about to end up with a ready-
made family?

#1109 TEMPORARILY HERS—Susan Meier
Bundles of Joy
Katherine Whitman was determined to win custody of her
nephew Jason—even if it meant a temporary marriage to playboy
Alex Cane. Then Katherine found herself falling for her new
"husband" and facing permanent heartache.

#1110 STAND-IN HUSBAND—Anne Peters
Pavel Mallik remembered nothing. All he knew was that the
lovely Marie Cooper had saved his life. Now he had the chance
to rescue her reputation by making her his wife!

#1111 STORYBOOK COWBOY—Pat Montana
Jo McPherson didn't trust Trey Covington. The handsome cowboy
brought back too many memories. Jo tried to resist his charm, but
Trey had his ways of making her forget the past…and dream about
the future.

#1112 FAMILY TIES—Dani Criss
Single mother Laine Sullivan knew Drew Casteel was commitment
shy. It would be smarter to steer clear of the handsome bachelor. But
Drew was hard to resist. Soon Laine had to decide whether or not to
risk her heart….

#1113 HONEYMOON SUITE—Linda Lewis
Premiere
Miranda St. James had always been pursued for her celebrity
connections. So when Stuart Winslow began to woo her, Miranda
kept her identity a secret. But Stuart had secrets of his own!

Become a Privileged Woman,
You'll be entitled to all these *Free Benefits.* And *Free Gifts,* too.

To thank you for buying our books, we've designed an exclusive FREE program called *PAGES & PRIVILEGES™*. You can enroll with just one Proof of Purchase, and get the kind of luxuries that, until now, you could only read about.

BIG HOTEL DISCOUNTS

A privileged woman stays in the finest hotels. And so can you—at up to 60% off! Imagine standing in a hotel check-in line and watching as the guest in front of you pays $150 for the same room that's only costing you $60. Your *Pages & Privileges* discounts are good at Sheraton, Marriott, Best Western, Hyatt and thousands of other fine hotels all over the U.S., Canada and Europe.

FREE DISCOUNT TRAVEL SERVICE

A privileged woman is always jetting to romantic places.

When <u>you</u> fly, just make one phone call for the lowest published airfare at time of booking— <u>or double the difference back!</u>

PLUS—you'll get a $25 voucher to use the first time you book a flight AND <u>5% cash back on every ticket you buy thereafter through the travel service!</u>